Anything Ghost

A Paranormal Cozy Mystery

Dina Marie

ISBN: 978-1-964858-05-0 (ebook)

ISBN: 978-1-964858-08-1 (paperback)

Book cover design by Elizabeth Mackey

For Mom

Chapter 1

"I KNOW I'M FORGETTING something ..."

I slipped my laptop computer into my briefcase and tossed in several pens and yellow legal pads for good measure. This visit to Las Vegas, part of the Salem Small Business Group's conference series, would be my first official business trip, and I wanted to look organized and professional. Even though I felt completely *un*organized and *un*professional. But my plan was to fake until I make it. Or so I told myself.

"Everything will be well, Clara," said William, who was standing nearby and looking at me kindly with his pale blue eyes. "No cause for worry."

"Thank you, William." William not only had a way of knowing just what I was thinking, but he also had a way of telling me exactly what I needed to hear. Even if I didn't believe it.

I glanced into my briefcase, having second thoughts about those pads and pens. *Does anyone use those anymore?* Would they make me look professional or old-fashioned? I giggled. I was definitely overthinking this.

I wiped a bit of dust off my new antique desk, the one piece of furniture I had treated myself to since moving to Kensington House. Other than a cot to sleep in and a goose-neck lamp I picked up from a flea market that had seen better days. I couldn't wait to start decorating in full force once the place was painted, the floors sanded, and whatever else the Salem Historical Society allowed me to do. I knew there were specific instructions on what I could and couldn't do with a historic home, but I hadn't realized they'd be so extensive. And monitored. Mavis was already threatening an unannounced visit. Like she was a social worker for child protective services.

"You will be away for seven days, yes?" William asked, poking at his phone. "I'd like to input it into my digital calendar."

I smiled. For a nineteenth-century ghost, William had taken to the cell phone I had given him for his birthday like a twenty-first-century middle schooler. Even after only a few weeks, he knew how to work it better than I did. And he was adopting the lingo. *Input? Digital calendar?* At this rate, soon he'd be telling me he wanted to slide into my DMs.

"Yes," I said. "Seven days, including travel days. The plan is to drive to the airport today and leave my car in long-term parking."

"And you will be flying in a fixed-wing flying machine?" he asked incredulously.

"Yes, an airplane." It must have seemed magical to William that humans took so easily to the air, like birds. The Wright brothers hadn't made their first successful powered flight until 1903 in Kitty Hawk, forty years after his death. Having a nineteenth-century friend made me realize how much humankind had progressed in the last hundred fifty years.

William pointed to his cell phone screen. "It states here airplane travel became commonplace in the 1950s and 1960s, a period oft referred to as the golden age of air travel."

"Yes, that's true. But remember what I said, William. You can't believe everything you read on the internet."

"Indeed. As per your suggestion, I am taking care to visit only reputable websites."

"Good plan." I looked around the room and at my luggage. "Well, I think I have what I need. Should we go over things again?"

"If it will ease your mind, then yes."

I had to laugh. William really *did* know me. "Okay." I glanced at my own digital calendar. "Later today, the painters are coming to the house to sand and tape and all that stuff."

"In other words, the painters will be arriving without paint and will not be painting."

"Exactly. Today is all about prep, and then tomorrow they will do all the painting. The day after that, internet is being installed and then the flooring people will be coming to sand and stain the floors. They should be finished in one day, possibly two." A nervous knot in my belly tightened. "I wish I could be here in case I'm needed, but this seemed to be the week that everyone was available. Go figure. If there's any problem at all, or if they seem confused, just text or call me. *Anytime.* Do you have any questions?"

"When I press the button bearing your name and telephone number, my message shall reach you all the way in Nevada, correct?" William asked. He had been excited to learn about Nevada when I showed it to him on a map; it had become a state the year following his death.

"Yes. I only added one phone number to your phone, so it should be pretty straight-forward. Remember, you can call or text me *anytime*." I had better leave; I was starting to sound like a parent leaving her teenager home alone for the first time.

"Very well." William adjusted his military jacket. "And as for the hound ..."

I loved it when William referred to Boy as a hound. It made him seem so regal.

"Are you certain you don't wish him to remain here while you are gone?" he asked.

Bark!

Boy was sitting next to my luggage, attentive, with my blond wig hanging out of his mouth, as if he, too, wanted to know why he couldn't just stay home during my trip.

"I wish I could, guys," I said, "but there's no way I can explain why I left my dog alone in the house." I bent down to scratch behind Boy's ears.

"He wouldn't be alone," William said somewhat indignantly.

"I know, but to others he *would* be, remember?" I reached down, picked up Boy, and cradled him in my arms. "Don't worry, little fella. Sebastian will take good care of you." He licked the tip of my nose.

I checked the bag I had packed for Boy to make sure I had his food bowls, his food, which was all portioned out for each day I was gone, and some of his toys. All looked well.

I was ready. At least on the outside. The inside remained to be seen.

"Well," I said, "I guess this is it."

On cue, Ghost Cat sashayed into the room from the wall separating the dining room and the living room with the timing of a seasoned theater actress.

"Did you come to see me off, too?" I asked her.

She walked toward the dining table, hopping on one of the chairs and then the table, peering into the bag with Boy's things. Then she sat on a placemat, blinking at me curiously. I reached over and held out my hand, and she nuzzled her little furry head into it.

"I'm sure you'll find things to keep you busy while Boy and me are gone," I told her, placing Boy down. Little did she know I had placed a few pens around for her to find and hide.

"If it is all right, Clara, I will depart," William said. "I'm not very fond of goodbyes." He bowed slightly. "I will keep you abreast of the goings-on here. Have a beneficial trip."

"Thank you. And remember, you can—"

"Call or text anytime, yes," William said as he faded from view.

I guess he knew that already. *I wonder why.* Could it have been the hundred times I told him?

I quickly brought my luggage and briefcase to the car and then came back and placed Boy's harness on, attaching his leash. Then I took one last look around the house. It was going to look very different when I returned. Walls painted. Floors sanded. A new TV. *Oh no, I forgot to mention the new TV to William.* So much change. For him. For me. I had to remind myself that change was good. That I was moving forward. That my new bed-and-breakfast was taking shape. And so was I. Still, I felt tears well in the corners of my eyes.

"It's just for a week," I said aloud. "You'll be back before you know it. Get a grip."

And with that, I picked up my purse and Boy's things and let Boy lead the way out the front door.

Chapter 2

I PARKED THE CAR in front of the *Salem Chronicle* office. Taylor Hampton hadn't returned any of my texts or calls for weeks, and since I had some time before I needed to get to the airport, I thought I would make an in-person attempt at communication.

I would have been lying if I'd said I was surprised Taylor was MIA. When I made the deal with him at Wyatt House—the identity of Kai Teller's murderer in return for helping me clear William's name of the false charges made against him over more than a century ago—I knew there was a good chance Taylor wouldn't follow through. *More* than a good chance. Taylor Hampton didn't care about anyone or anything but himself. I didn't know him too well, but I knew *that* about him. But if Taylor thought I was the kind of girl who would just let him roll over me, then he didn't really know *me* too well. I wasn't letting anyone—especially a man—roll over me anymore. And *ghosting* I was beginning to learn how to handle.

"C'mon, Boy," I said. "Let's go track down a narcissist."

Bark!

The vertical blinds across the *Salem Chronicle*'s two large windows were closed, and I tried the doorknob of the wooden door, but it was locked. A sign was posted on the clear glass:

The Salem Chronicle office will be closed until noon as star reporter Taylor Hampton has a speaking engagement at Salem High School, where he'll be instructing the newspaper staff on the finer points of investigation.

Oh, brother.

It was clear that Taylor had written the sign himself.

I peered inside the office, wondering if maybe I might see Taylor's boss, Mabel Eckers, the *Chronicle*'s longtime editor. If Taylor wasn't going to search the newspaper's archives, then maybe Mabel would help. But the lights were off and everything was still. No one was there.

"No luck, Boy," I said, looking down at my Shih Tzu's cute little black-and-white face. "Taylor Hampton has managed to evade us once again."

Bark!

Boy circled the sidewalk a couple of times and then peed right on the *Salem Chronicle* doorstep.

"Right on, Boy," I said with a giggle. I looked at my watch. "C'mon, let's walk to The Pampered Pup."

When we arrived, Sebastian was standing at the front counter and talking to a client, who was holding a nervous Yorkie in her arms.

"It'll be okay, Oreo," Sebastian was saying. "You've been here before, and everything was all right." He reached out to pet the dog's head.

Kind, gentle Sebastian. If there was a perfect person to watch Boy for a week, it was definitely him. When Sebastian's hand touched the top of the dog's head, the dog stopped shaking for a moment but resumed when he took his hand away. Sebastian gently picked the dog out of the owner's hands. "I'll see you in about an hour and a half, Mrs. Moran," he said. The owner nodded before she turned around, smiled at me, and strode out the door.

"Clara, hey," Sebastian said when he saw me.

"What an adorable dog!" I said, glancing at Oreo.

Bark!

"Oh, of course, you're adorable, too, Boy." I petted his overgrown, hairy head.

"Oreo is not a fan of getting his hair cut. He's been coming here for years but gets so nervous. I end up holding him most of the time."

"You're so good with dogs," I said.

"Well, I've been doing this for a while. You get to learn what every dog needs. Excuse me one second." Sebastian slipped into the back and came out with his hands free. "Hey, Boy, how's it going?!"

Bark!

"That's good to hear!" Sebastian said with a laugh. "We're gonna have fun this week."

"Now you be a good boy for Sebastian, okay?"

Boy walked straight into the little corral section of the store. I handed Sebastian the leash and placed Boy's bag on the front counter. "Okay," I said, "so you have all his food, and I've portioned it out for you, so you only have to open each plastic baggie and dump it into his bowl. He gets the dry kibble and a sixth of the wet food container. I've even pre-cut the wet food halfway for you."

"I see that," Sebastian said with a smile as he looked into the bag.

"Overkill?"

"Maybe a little." He laughed.

"I can't help it. This is the first time I've left him alone for more than a few hours." My throat tightened a little. "And I brought his second and third favorite toys. I didn't want to bring his favorite—my old blond wig—because I thought that might be a little weird, so I brought his woolly mammoth and blue bone." I fished around in the bag. "And in case he gets a little hungry between meals, I brought—"

"He'll be okay, Clara." Sebastian gently took the bag from the counter and placed it on a shelf. "I'll take good care of him. I promise."

"I know you will." I swallowed, hoping the lump in my throat would go away. It didn't.

"So, are you all set for your big trip? Las Vegas is one of those cities that never sleeps. There's lots to do."

I knew Sebastian was trying to change the subject. And I appreciated it. "Ready as I'll ever be, I guess. I'm excited but a bit nervous about flying."

"Have you ever flown in a plane before?"

"Not for about ten years. The last flight I took was to the island of Grenada in the Caribbean." With Joe. And if I had been smart, I would have run away from him then when I had the chance.

"Well, nothing much has changed. Put on a good movie, and you'll be fine. And you'll have a lot of fun in Vegas. Be sure to see some of the sights while you're there. And who knows, maybe you'll make some friends."

Bark!

Boy put his little paws on the corral gate separating us and gazed at me through the slats.

Ugh. It looked like he was in prison. *Don't make this even harder, little one.*

"I'd better go before I burst into tears." I gave Boy a big kiss on the top of his head. "Thanks again, Sebastian." Without thinking, I leaned in for a hug and felt Sebastian's arms wrap around me. They felt safe. Warm.

When we parted, Sebastian looked like he wanted to say something, but he just nodded. "Anytime. I'll send pictures throughout the week so you don't worry."

I'll probably worry anyway. "Okay." Then I waved goodbye to Sebastian and my dog and strode toward the exit without looking back, bracing myself for my first official business trip.

Chapter 3

Airport security took way longer than I thought it would. I had given myself extra time to check my bag, but I hadn't planned on getting randomly selected for additional screening. And now I was running down those moving escalators like a lunatic, the strap of my briefcase wrapped around me like a messenger bag because, as luck would have it, my gate was at the far end of the airport.

Thankfully, when I reached the gate, most of the passengers were still seated, scrolling on their phones and entertaining children. I spotted Sissy near the window. Away from Haute Chocolate, she seemed out of place, like a grade-school teacher at the supermarket. When she saw me, she waved.

"Coming!" I called.

Travel Mistake #1: Yelling.

Just about every passenger seated in the vicinity looked up at me with curiosity and/or annoyance. Somehow, I was still managing to draw attention to myself, whether I was running away or running *anywhere*.

Sissy was sitting with Stephanie, Alice, and two men I recognized from the Salem Small Business Group meeting, all their luggage congregated in the center of their circle.

"Hey, lady!" Stephanie said. "I wasn't sure if you were going to make it." She was wearing that colorful Jackson Pollack-esque jacket she had on when we first met.

"There was traffic, and then I got pulled for additional screening."

"I hate when that happens," said the hazel-eyed guy sitting next to Sissy. He stood and held out his hand. "Hi, I'm Declan." I shook it.

"Declan owns Salem Blooms," Sissy said. "It's a family-owned business that's been a staple in Salem since the eighties. I can't think of a wedding that I've been to in the past twenty years that *hasn't* used Declan for their bouquets and table centerpieces. He's got an amazing eye." She pointed to the other gentleman. "And I'm not sure if you know Jonah Duncan, one of the owners of the newly opened Salem Seas. It's a seafood restaurant."

"Nice to meet you, Jonah."

It wasn't until Jonah stood to shake my hand that I realized how big and tall he was. Like a grizzly, although somewhat less cuddly.

"And I believe you already know Alice." Sissy motioned toward Alice, who, not surprisingly, was sitting off to the side, her body shifted away from the others. Alice's eyes met mine briefly.

"Nice to see you again, Alice," I said, sitting in a vacant seat.

Alice nodded shyly, her eyes flicking to mine behind her large, rimmed glasses and then returning to her e-reader. Apparently, not much had changed since I last saw her a month ago at Wyatt House. I thought maybe a murder investigation would have bonded us.

"Good afternoon," said a voice coming from an overheard speaker. I looked toward the gate and saw a young woman with a pixie haircut speaking into a microphone. "On behalf of Delta Airlines, it is my pleasure to welcome you to Flight 732 to Las Vegas. We would like to now begin pre-boarding those passengers requiring special assistance."

Part of me wanted to stand up and make my way to the gate. I needed all the special assistance I could get for this trip.

"So, how's the bed-and-breakfast prep going?" Stephanie asked.

"You're opening a bed-and-breakfast?" Declan asked me. "How fun."

"Yeah." Little did he know I was responding to his first sentence, not agreeing with his second. "I'm hoping to open for the October season."

"That's only two months away," Jonah said, stirring up the nervous butterflies already in my insides.

"She'll be ready." Stephanie patted my knee. "It's going to be great."

I was happy Stephanie was on this trip. She exuded positivity. And, like William, she always gave me the feeling I knew what I was doing.

Static resumed overhead, and the pixie-haired airline worker returned to her microphone. "We're now going to begin boarding our first-class and business-class passengers, as well as our SkyMiles members."

That was quick. *I guess no one needs special assistance.*

Jonah and Declan reached for their luggage.

"Wow, first class, huh, guys?" Stephanie asked with raised eyebrows.

"I only travel first class," Jonah said. "I'm a big guy, and for me, it's worth the expense."

"I don't know if I can say the same," Declan said with a laugh, motioning toward his shorter—maybe five-foot-nine—stature. "I had some SkyMiles, so I upgraded." He shrugged.

"Sure," Stephanie said, "leave us in coach with the rest of steerage and go have your free cocktails and extra leg room. See if I care." She smiled.

Declan's cheeks turned a pale shade of red, and I thought I detected a lingering glance between him and Stephanie. "Well, I guess we'll see you all in Vegas," he said.

"Yes, let's meet at baggage claim," said Sissy, the leader of our little crew.

Declan nodded, and he and Jonah took off for the passenger boarding bridge.

"He seems like a nice guy. Declan," I said to Stephanie.

"Oh?" she asked innocently. "I hadn't noticed." We both smiled.

"So, what do you hope to learn during this trip, Clara?" Sissy asked.

"Well … as much as I can, I guess. It wasn't until my event at Wyatt House that I realized how much I *don't* know. I majored in hospitality and tourism in college, but so much has changed in the past ten years. I feel like I'm starting from scratch."

"You'll pick it up," Stephanie said with assurance.

"Agreed. And we're all here to help one another," Sissy said. "That's the motto of the SSBG. A rising tide lifts all boats."

"Yeah, well, some of us need a life preserver," I said. Out of the corner of my eye, I thought I saw Alice smile a little at my joke, but I couldn't be sure.

When the line of passengers had shortened to only a few, the pixie-haired lady returned to the microphone. "We are now ready to begin the general boarding process. Boarding first, Group A."

"That's me," Sissy said.

"Same," Stephanie said. "What group are you, Clara?"

I looked at the boarding pass on my phone. "Yep, Group A, too."

"Hey, you're in 12C," Stephanie said, glancing at my boarding pass. "I'm 12D. Right across the aisle."

"How about you, Alice?" I asked.

"I'm Group A, also," she said timidly, showing us her phone screen.

"Hey, Alice, you're right behind me in row thirteen." Stephanie tilted Alice's phone toward her. "I hope you're not a seat-kicker."

Alice's cheeks flushed, as if she was mortified by the insinuation.

"I'm just kidding," Stephanie said. "C'mon, let's go. My money is burning a hole in my pocket. Can't wait to play some craps."

As we joined the line and inched closer to the plane door, excitement bubbled up inside me. I was finally going *somewhere*. A place I had never been.

"I'm so excited," I blurted. "I haven't traveled very much."

"Well, you're starting off with a whopper," Sissy said. "Las Vegas is one of a kind."

"Yeah, it can be a bit overwhelming," Stephanie said, "but by the end of the trip, you'll be a Vegas pro."

As we shuffled toward the plane, my phone pinged, and I smiled. I knew it was William. I had selected a classical music sequence as his notification ringtone. I clicked on his text.

Dear Clara,

I smiled wider, loving the formality. You can bring the nineteenth-century man into the twenty-first century, but there were some things you couldn't change. Nor would I want to.

The letter you left for the painter, while very clear to me, has him puzzled. Before you "take off," as is commonplace to say in your century, on your flying machine, would you kindly phone him and confirm that you would like crème, not green, in the kitchen?
Sincerely,
William

A pang of guilt shot through me for not being at Kensington House during the renovations. But I took a deep breath, reminding myself to relax, that everything would be okay. I replied to William's text, letting him know I would contact the painter, and quickly shot a text to the painter. Then I put my phone in airplane mode and shoved it into my purse, hoping whatever other questions there were could wait for about five hours.

"So?" Stephanie asked as we moved closer to the plane.

"So, what?"

"So? Who's William?"

My body stiffened. *She read my text?* "Oh, um," I stammered. "He's ..."

"Sorry, I didn't mean to snoop," she said, "but the text seemed to give you so much joy. And the writing is so formal! How early eighteen hundreds!"

Actually, it's late eighteen hundreds.

"Well," Stephanie blinked, "is this a new beau?"

"Um ..." *How to explain William?* "No, he's a friend." Not a lie. "A *good* friend." Still not a lie. "He's helping me with facilitating the work in the bed-and-breakfast while I'm traveling." *I'm on a truth-telling roll!*

"Oh, I see. *Just a friend.*" Stephanie playfully jabbed her elbow into my side. "Got it."

Travel Mistake #2: Reading texts from your ghost friend in public.

We finally boarded the plane and made our way to our seats, saying a quick hi to Jonah and Declan, who looked more relaxed and comfortable than airline passengers should. I slipped into my suddenly too-cramped-looking aisle seat and shoved my briefcase and purse into the space under the seat in front of me.

"Ready?" Stephanie asked, buckling her seatbelt.

"Ready." I fastened mine and plugged in my headphones, excitedly scrolling through the movie selections, as Sebastian suggested. Soon, the flight attendants secured all the overhead bins and, as the plane taxied toward the runway, went through all the security measures.

Sebastian was right. Not much had changed in the ten years since I'd flown. The closest exit on the plane might be behind me. Life preservers were still under the seats. Mothers were still being instructed to secure their own oxygen masks before their children's, should they fall from the ceiling when the air pressure dropped. All of which made me feel like I hadn't missed that much in the time I was playing housewife to Joe.

Then before I knew it, the engines roared, and I gripped my arm rests. *This is it.* I thought of all the travel posters hanging in my bedroom when I was growing up. All the places I intended to go. All the plans I had made. It had taken eight years, but I had finally gotten out from under the thumb of the person who was supposed to be my copilot, and I was finally going to see one of the many extraordinary places on this wonderful planet.

As the plane's wheels lifted from the ground and this giant hunk of metal soared into the sky, I tried to remember everything I was feeling so that, seven days from now, I could go home, curl up on the couch with my dog and ghost cat, and tell William all about it.

Chapter 4

Wow.

That's all I could think as I looked out the window of our taxi as we drove down Las Vegas Boulevard toward our hotel. I was no stranger to bright lights and big cities, having been raised just a train ride from New York City, but Las Vegas was Times Square on steroids.

The look of astonishment must have been evident on my face because the Uber driver asked me, "This is your first time to Vegas?"

"Yeah, she's a virgin," Stephanie said. I elbowed her playfully.

"Here's a tip from me: don't get distracted by the shiny penny." The driver raised his eyebrows and twitched his bushy mustache as he made a turn. "I know it looks glamorous and all, but it's a fake city. Things aren't always what they seem."

Stephanie and I looked at one another.

"I pick people up from the airport who come here from all over the world," the driver continued. "They come for football, gambling, shows, racing, whatever. And they have the same look as you have right now. But let me tell you ..." He stopped at a red light and turned to look back at me. "A lot of them don't look so bright-eyed when they go back to the airport."

Boy, this guy definitely didn't work for the Las Vegas Convention and Visitors Authority.

"You sound like a guy who lost his shirt at the casino," Jonah said with a laugh.

"I lost more than that in Vegas, my friend," the driver said, pulling into the hotel's long driveway. "Why do you think I'm driving a cab?"

He came to a stop in front of glass doors that looked like they were the entrance to Oz. A long red carpet led up to them, like the kind rolled out for celebrities. As we exited the vehicle, the intense heat that greeted me at the airport again slapped me in the face. I knew Las Vegas had what they called a dry heat, but, wet or dry, it felt like I was baking at 400 degrees Fahrenheit.

The driver helped us pull our luggage from the trunk. Mine was the last one out, and when he handed it to me, he looked me in the eye. "Didn't mean to scare you," he said.

"No, you didn't scare me." He had no idea of the kind of scary stuff I was used to.

"Don't mind me. I'm an old, disgruntled, divorced re-formed gambler." He handed me my bag. "Enjoy yourself. But not *too* much."

"Thanks so much for the ride!" Stephanie said, pulling me away from him. She hooked her arm with mine and walked with me on the red carpet. "Well, *that* was depressing," she said as a doorman opened one of those towering glass doors for us and we entered the lobby. "Remind me to one-star that guy and not request him on the way back to the air-port."

I had a hard time hearing her as we walked into the ho-tel. The noise level of our surroundings suddenly jumped a bunch of decibels. Slot machines dinged. Roulette wheels spun as a trio of showgirls paraded by in crystal headdresses, jeweled bra tops, and little else. Craps players alternately shouted in delight or despair as lights blinked, and my nos-trils burned from cigarette smoke. I had stumbled into a never-ending nightlife while, outside, the sun was still up, although you wouldn't know it because there were no win-dows to be found.

I thought of home, of Salem, where it was quiet and prob-ably dark by now, and of William and what he might think of this place. At first glance, Las Vegas would probably be over-whelming for a guy from the eighteen hundreds. Because it was pretty overwhelming to twenty-first-century me.

After waiting in line to check in, Stephanie and I walked over to a registration booth located near an all-night bakeshop, where Sissy, Alice, Jonah, and Declan were standing. A banner read *Business Start-Up 101: Everything You Wanted to Know About Starting a Business and Were Afraid to Ask.*

"Check in here, and we'll meet by the elevators," Sissy said.

I liked Sissy. Traveling with her reminded me of family vacations with my mom.

After Stephanie and I got our welcome materials and badges, which made me feel so official, we met up with the rest of our group by the elevators.

"All right," Sissy said. "Welcome to Las Vegas, everyone. As noted in the emails you should have received from the conference organizers, there will be a welcome reception tonight on the twenty-seventh floor. From what I gather, most of the conference will take place on the twenty-seventh floor, what they call the Royal Suite of Rooms. It's a nice space with a lovely balcony. I've been there before. The opening-night cocktail reception begins in a few hours, at six p.m., and there's a dinner theater show as well, I believe. You might want to bring a wrap or sweater, ladies. It can get chilly."

"But it's over a hundred degrees outside," Stephanie said. "How cold can it be on a balcony?"

Sissy shook her head. "I wasn't talking about the balcony. The rooms themselves are practically refrigerated. The balcony is where people go to get a reprieve!" She laughed. "Also, security tends to be tight in these hotels, so you'll need to wear your badges." She pointed to the badge in my hand. "Be sure you wear it tonight."

"But it doesn't go with my cocktail dress," Stephanie said with a pouty face.

"Do the best you can," Sissy said.

We piled our luggage into the elevator, which was the size of a small apartment. On the third floor, Jonah, Sissy, and Declan got off.

"See you in a few," Declan said, mostly to Stephanie, as the door closed behind him.

"What floor are you guys?" Stephanie asked Alice and me.

"Fifth," I said.

Alice nodded. "Me too."

"Same!" Stephanie squealed. "Maybe we can have a slumber party one night while we're here."

I couldn't imagine Alice wanting anything to do with a slumber party. I looked back at her. She was studying the ascending numbers of the elevator as if her life depended on them.

When the elevator door opened again, I stepped out and glanced at the hotel directory in front of us.

"I'm five-forty. This way," Stephanie said, pointing to the right.

"I'm five-twenty-one." I pointed the other way.

"Oh, darn. How about you, Alice?"

"Five-twenty-two," she said.

"Wow, you guys are probably right across from one another. You better have no slumber parties without me!" She giggled. "See you in a few hours!" With that, she glided down the hallway toward her room.

As soon as Stephanie left, it was like she took all the air in the hallway with her. I stood awkwardly with Alice, not sure of what to say, but before I could get out a proper "um," Alice started lugging her stuff toward our rooms, and I just followed behind.

"It'll be nice to have someone I know nearby," I said, knowing it was a weak conversation starter.

"Mmm hmmm," Alice said.

She never said much but always managed to say *just enough* so that she didn't appear rude. It was quite impressive actually.

When we got to our rooms, Stephanie was right. My room and Alice's were right across the hallway from one another.

"I guess I'll see you in a bit," I said, holding my key card up and activating my hotel door's lock.

She nodded and gave a timid "okay" before disappearing behind her hotel door. *And locking her deadbolt.*

I tried not to take it personally that Alice thought I might want to break into her room. Instead, I walked into my own room and closed the door behind me.

The hotel room wasn't anything special. It looked like probably every other room I'd been in while on vacation of some sort—or being held hostage by Joe. Two full-size beds. Desk. Table. Lamps that I could never figure out how to turn on.

But something was different.

I have it all to myself.

The curtains were open, and I gazed out the window at the Las Vegas afternoon. In the distance, the Sphere, one of Las Vegas's newest attractions, looked like a giant meteor that landed smack dab in the middle of the city. It was smiling at me with a big, yellow face. I smiled back and turned around and faced my room.

I wanted to unzip my suitcase, dump all the contents onto the bed, and fill all the drawers of the furniture. Joe never wanted me to do that. Never wanted me to take up space. He always said he needed the closets for his work clothing and the drawers for his shirts so they didn't wrinkle. I was always left having to live out of my suitcase.

I reached for my phone and took it off airplane mode, and a few text messages popped in. Two were from William.

Dear Clara,

As expected, the painter performed no painting today but used quite a large amount of tape and a white substance to fill holes. He also used a device that, according to my internet research, is an electric sander, which helped to flatten the uneven parts. Such contrivances! I'll have more to report to-morrow. Are you still flying through the air like a bird? It is dumbfounding how so many people can be carried in such a way.

Sincerely,

William

Something told me that I would probably never delete any of William's texts. I wanted to put them in a museum. The second one had a photo attached: an image of the dining room wall that had been taped and spackled.

Dear Clara,

I am afraid Ghost Cat appears fascinated by the tape used by the painter near the bottom of this wall and has been pulling at its corner, unraveling it slightly. I endeavored to repair it, but I fear my attempt may not prove adequate. Perhaps the painter will not pay it any mind. In any case, I am enclosing a photo of Ghost Cat in front of this wall—the culprit and the scene of the crime.

Sincerely,

William

I giggled. Ghost Cat was up to her tricks again. I zoomed in on the photo William sent, but Ghost Cat was nowhere in sight. Hmmm ... another vampire-like quality. Not only did ghosts have to be invited into your home, but they didn't show up in photography. Thank goodness they didn't suck people's blood.

I quickly texted William that I had arrived safely and not to sweat the painting tape. Then I took a photo of my room and the view from my room, including the Sphere, and sent it to him with the message: *I can't wait to tell you all about it!*

The time stamp on my phone screen told me I had about two hours until the cocktail party. Just enough time to put my clothing away, shower, and change. But first I was going to do what any serious adult would do when finding herself alone in a hotel room for the very first time on her very first business trip.

I leaped on top of the bed closest to me and began jumping on it as high as I could as the yellow-faced Sphere smiled at me with approval.

Chapter 5

I TWIRLED IN FRONT of the closet's mirrored sliding door, admiring my black cocktail dress. It had been a long time since I had a reason to dress up. And it had been even longer since I *enjoyed* dressing up. When married to Joe, I liked to stay under the radar when it came to parties and tended to dress a little conservatively. I never wanted to give him a reason to look at me, but he had a habit of dragging me to business functions as much as possible so he could dress me up like a doll and parade me around to all his colleagues.

Like I was there for his enjoyment.

And amusement.

I cleared him from my mind. Enough of that. Finally, I was dressing for me. The way *I* wanted.

I was about to do another twirl in the other direction when there was a knock on my door. I looked through the peephole and smiled.

"Well, don't you look pretty!" Stephanie said when I opened the door.

"Thanks! So do you!" I said, admiring her ruffle-sleeved blue sheath wrap. "I love the color. Come on in. I'm almost ready."

Stephanie stepped inside.

"I'll just be a minute." I went into the bathroom and applied a bit of mascara to my eyes, nearly blinding myself with the applicator because I was so out of practice. I couldn't remember the last time I had worn makeup. I never really was a glam girl, but I used to like to wear makeup for special occasions—at least before I was married. "Should we get Alice, too?" I asked.

"We could, but I think Alice likes to make an entrance alone. I usually try not to overwhelm her. I think I may have with the slumber party suggestion."

I smiled. "I think she'll be okay." I twisted the mascara applicator closed when a familiar strain of classical music emanated into the room.

Oh no. My phone.

"You're getting a text," Stephanie said. "Ah, it's that guy William again."

Low-key panic. Flooding through me. *Oh, who am I kidding?* The panic was definitely *high-key*. There was no telling what William might have written. Something about the painters? Or something to do with haunting Kensington House for a hundred fifty years and a Ghost Cat who liked to undo painting tape?

I leaped out of the bathroom and then nonchalantly reached for my phone. "Yeah, he's giving me updates on the painters." No big deal. Just a normal day in a normal world. Not a paranormal day in a paranormal world.

"Wow, you trust him enough to leave him alone in your house, huh?" She smiled. "I'd say this William guy is sounding like much more than just a friend."

"Well, he's a *good* friend."

"I should say so."

In a lame attempt to change the subject, I pointed to my phone screen. "Wow, look at the time. We'd better get going. We don't want to be late."

"Damn right. Bring on the hors d'oeuvres!"

When the elevator doors opened on the twenty-seventh floor, a flurry of excitement greeted us. Men and women dressed for a party and talking animatedly. Waiters weaving from group to group with trays topped with glass flutes filled with what looked like champagne.

"Wow, this is so fancy," I said. "Is this all for the conference?"

"Yeah. That's probably why the conference fee was so high. Better get our money's worth." Stephanie grabbed two flutes of champagne from a passing waiter. "For you, made-moiselle."

"Why thank you!" I took a sip, and the bubbles tickled the bottom of my nose. "I don't really drink much." I always had to stay on my toes around Joe. "Just never developed a taste for it, I guess."

"Unfortunately, I *have* developed a taste for it." Stephanie took another sip that was more like a gulp as we walked out of the elevator area toward the main room. About fifteen tables were set up, each sporting long white tablecloths and place settings for six to ten people.

"Look, there's Sissy!" Stephanie said.

I spotted her in the crowd. Sissy looked beautiful in an understated forest green sequined A-line dress. Her hair was pulled back from her face, and she wore dark eyeshadow that brought out the deep brown of her eyes. She was standing near one of the round tables that had the words *Salem Small Business Group* on a placard at the center, atop a floral centerpiece.

"Don't you ladies look lovely," Sissy said.

"I'll second that," Declan said, raising his glass. He had been standing beside Sissy and was wearing a gray suit with a maroon tie. His eyes met Stephanie's. They toasted.

"We're missing two," Sissy said.

"Here comes Alice," Stephanie said.

Alice was trying to excuse her way toward our table but got caught between two men who appeared not to have seen each other in years and were wrapped in a bear hug. They each had about a hundred pounds on Alice, who looked like a sliver of Swiss cheese between two thick pieces of bread. She turned beet red, eventually escaping their clutches, and hurried to our table.

"You look so pretty, Alice," I said. She was wearing a black cocktail dress similar to mine. I couldn't recall ever seeing Alice without her apron. She appeared uncomfortable by my compliment, but in polite Alice fashion, she uttered a quiet "thank you" before her eyes found the floor.

"I think Jonah is over there, by the bar," Declan said. He pointed to an outdoor section of the floor, where there was a balcony and a wonderful view of the hotels along Las Vegas Boulevard.

"That's a good place to be," Stephanie said, downing her champagne and placing it on an empty tray as a waiter zoomed past us. "Anyone else want anything? It's on me!" She giggled.

"I'm good," I said, as did the others, and Stephanie went off happily toward the bar.

Sissy and Declan resumed the conversation they had been having when we walked over, which left Alice and me standing next to each other awkwardly. I knew there was a ten-year-ish age difference between us, but I should have been able to figure out how to relate to a twenty-two-year-old woman—even if she was shy. *How hard can it be?*

"Have you been to Las Vegas before, Alice?"

"No." She shook her head, her eyes meeting mine for the tiniest of fractions.

"Me either. First time." I nodded.

Silence.

"For a while there," I continued, "when I was seventeen, I thought about going to college in Las Vegas. The University of Nevada has a college of hospitality, and I figured where better to learn the tourism trade than one of the most tourist-filled cities in the country, right?"

Silence.

"But I ended up going to a state school in New York instead. Where did you go to college, Alice?"

"UMass," she said, but nothing more.

"Did you like it?"

"It was all right."

"What did you major in?"

"Business."

"When did you graduate?"

"December of last year." She leaned down, reached for a glass of water on the table, and took a sip as if the constant talking was getting her parched.

"Do you like working at The Haunted Cookie?" I asked when she put the glass down.

"It's all right."

I nodded. I wasn't getting anywhere. And I felt like I was interrogating her.

Luckily, a man dressed in a sharp navy-blue suit stepped onto a circular stage that had been erected on the dance floor in the middle of the room and tapped a microphone, saving me from harassing Alice any longer.

"Attention, ladies and gentlemen," he said. "Please take your seats. We have a special performance this evening to kick off our exciting conference. We'll be starting in about ten minutes or so." Instantly, the dozens of people who had been standing in the elevator lobby and on the balcony began walking into the room, looking for their tables.

Alice was looking off into the room, and I was thinking about taking a walk to give Alice a break when someone said, "So, you're opening a bed-and-breakfast, too."

I turned and in front of me was a man who looked to be in his late thirties. Light brown eyes. Short brown hair. A strong, self-assured chin. (Kind of like Joe's, but I didn't want to hold that against him.) I glanced at his conference badge, which read *Glenn Swanson, Swanson's Bed-and-Breakfast, Las Vegas, Nevada.*

"Guilty," I said. "It's nice to know I'm not the only crazy one."

Glenn Swanson laughed, revealing a pair of dimples on both cheeks. "Nah, someone here is opening an internet café, which is pretty crazy. Isn't that just a café?"

I laughed. "Well, technically, I guess I'm opening an internet bed-and-breakfast since I plan on giving Wi-Fi access to my guests."

"You know, you make a good point. I'm opening an internet B&B as well." He stuck out his hand. "Hi, I'm Glenn Swanson."

I shook it. "Clara Kelly. Have you ever been to one of these things? It's my first time."

"I've been to a few. I think you'll find them helpful. Kurt puts on a good show." He glanced at my dress in a way that showed approval, and I wasn't sure how I felt about that. I was so used to not wanting to attract attention, especially from men, but at the same time, it was nice to have a man notice my effort. Darn Joe. Still haunting me from the grave. "When do you plan on opening your bed-and-breakfast?" he asked.

"In October. Sometimes I wonder if I'm going too fast, but that's our busy season."

"Right, Salem. Gotta get in on those Halloween buffs. Better brush up on your ghost stories."

Already have. Check. I smiled.

"Shall we sit?" Sissy asked, pulling out one of the chairs.

"Well, I'll let you get to it," Glenn said. "It was very nice meeting you."

"You as well," I said as he walked away.

I took the seat closest to me and tried not to take it personally that Alice sat clear on the other side of the table. She might not have said much during our little chat, but between this and the deadbolted hotel door, I definitely was getting the hint. *Less Clara.*

Stephanie and Jonah returned from the bar with drinks in their hands, and Stephanie took the seat next to me on the right.

"Don't think I didn't see you chatting with that hot guy," she said to me as Jonah took the seat on the other side of her. I detected a definite slur in her speech.

"He's opening a bed-and-breakfast," I said.

"Right. And *that's* why you were talking with him." She over-giggled, clearly tipsy.

"Is this seat taken?" Declan asked me, indicating the seat on my left. He glanced at Jonah, who had taken the seat next to Stephanie. I didn't mind being the consolation prize. I smiled. "It's all yours."

Stephanie reached for the menu that had been placed on the plate in front of her. "It's quite a selection. I might order the duck."

I had already decided I would stick to the basics. No need to rile up my already nervous stomach. It would be salmon or chicken. Probably salmon, a tiny salute to my dad and his famous salmon meatballs. I reached for my compass pendant around my neck and rubbed it.

"What a beautiful necklace," Declan said.

"Thanks. My dad gave it to me when I got my first job."

"Is that a Celtic design?"

"It is!" I pointed to the eight-pointed shape at the pendant's center. "That's the Vegvísir. It's a Norse protection symbol. It's supposed to keep a person from getting lost.

And it's also got a Western-style compass, too. North. South. East. West."

"It's like the best of both worlds."

"That's what *he* said." I smiled, although I could feel the tears welling in my eyes. I missed my dad.

The server came and took our drink orders, and then the man who had been on stage before returned. I realized that I recognized him from the conference website. If I remembered correctly, his name was Kurt Walker. He ran several small companies in the tech field before selling them for millions of dollars and starting up this series of conferences. He also taught business at the University of Nevada in Las Vegas.

"Welcome, everyone! If you don't know me by now, my name is Kurt Walker. I'm your head bottle washer, and I am thrilled you could join us this week for this wonderful conference we're calling Business 101: Everything You Wanted to Know About Starting a Business and Were Afraid to Ask."

"I'm afraid to ask!" someone shouted from one of the tables, and everyone laughed.

"No worries, my friend! We're going to tell you anyway! We have a variety of business professionals who are taking time off from their busy schedules this week to present panels on many topics. As the conference literature states, whether you're just starting out or a business veteran, we guarantee you'll learn something this week that you can go home and apply to your business right now."

"I know absolutely nothing, so I'm sure to learn something this week," I said.

"Clara, you know more than you think," Stephanie said. "You've got good instincts."

"And that's all you need, really," Declan noted. "Everything else you can figure out."

"Exactly," Stephanie said, nodding at Declan.

He nodded, and their eyes met again.

If the three of us were some kind of grade-school science project of an electric circuit, I was feeling more and more like the rubber stopper in the middle.

"Tonight's more pleasure than business, though," Kurt Walker said, pointing to one of the tables in the back. "My wife, Deidre, is joining me again for this conference. Married ten years this week. I love you, honey!"

A collective *awww* rose from the crowd.

"All right, everyone, I hope you're ready to get the party started!"

The audience clapped wildly, and Stephanie stuck two fingers in her mouth and whistled.

"Great!" Kurt said. "It seems like you're warmed up! A bit of housekeeping, first. Please let your waitstaff know if there are any allergy or dietary concerns this evening. We want everyone healthy and happy. And then we only have one other rule here at our Business Start-Up 101 conferences. And that's to have fun!"

"You don't have to tell me twice!" Stephanie said, reaching for her drink.

"That's the spirit!" Kurt Walker called to our table. "Those of you who have attended our conferences before know we like to keep our groups on the small and manageable side. We don't give presentations in giant ballrooms with rows and rows of seating. We pride ourselves on giving business owners that intimate, special touch. And speaking of special ... As your servers come around to take your orders, we have a special treat for you. What would Las Vegas be without a show, right?!"

More hooting and hollering from the audience. I had a feeling the noise level would be commensurate with the number of free drinks making their way to the dinner tables.

"There are many names associated with Las Vegas," Kurt Walker said. "Frank Sinatra. Wayne Newton. Celine Dion. And also the superstar who is about to grace this stage."

More oohs and aahs from the audience.

"This award-winning stage actress," Kurt continued, "has been hailed as the theater performer of the twentieth century by *Playbill* magazine, and we are thrilled to say that she is here tonight to perform the song that skyrocketed her to fame when she sang it on Broadway in the nineties. I'm sure you all know it ... 'Anything Goes,' from the Cole Porter musical of the same name and for which she won a Tony

Award for the musical's revival. Please join me in giving a warm welcome to the one ... the only ... Angela Decatur!"

A woman who must have been in her seventies stepped out from the balcony. She was wearing a long, sequined gold gown that swished as she walked and looked like it must have weighed about twenty pounds.

"Do you know her?" Declan whispered to me.

I shook my head. I knew the musical *Anything Goes*. I was a pretty big theatergoer as a kid—my mom would even take me out of school for a mother-daughter excursion into New York City to see a matinee from time to time. But Angela Decatur? Not really. I wondered if my parents would have known her.

When Angela reached the stage, she gave Kurt her hand, old-school style, as if she expected him to kiss it, and then she glided to center stage, taking a bow, as the audience cheered. A few of the older gentlemen in the crowd were even standing, stars in their eyes.

"How old is she?" Jonah whispered.

"I think she has to be in her seventies by now," Sissy said. "I actually saw her in that *Anything Goes* production in the nineties. She was fantastic."

Men and women, dressed in sailor outfits, ran from the balcony to the stage, posing in a variety of ways behind Angela Decatur. They looked like some kind of live-action art exhibit.

"And now I give you," Kurt said dramatically, "Angela Decatur and company." Then he quickly left the stage as the lights dimmed, and a spotlight shined on Angela.

"Excuse me, ma'am," someone said, tapping my shoulder.

I looked up into the face of a young man dressed in a black jacket, white dress shirt, black pants, and a black tie. I realized it was my waiter. "Hi," I said.

"Have you decided on dinner, ma'am?" he whispered.

"Oh, yes, I'll take the salmon, please. Thank you."

"Any allergies?"

"No, none at all," I whispered as the familiar opening notes of "Anything Goes" began to play and the waiter moved on to Stephanie. The men and women behind Angela Decatur began to sway, and then the renowned theater actress took a step forward and began to sing.

I couldn't take my eyes off her. She commanded the stage with grace and elegance. As the rest of the company performed all kinds of steps behind her—from swing to tap—she moved slowly and deliberately, from one end of the stage to another, as if singing for each audience member individually. The seasoned performer. In those hooded eyes and lined face, I could see decades of soul-baring soliloquies executed on stages across the world. Angela Decatur might not have had the energy of the younger dancers surrounding her, but she had that star quality—that somethin' somethin' that makes a performer seem not of this earth. (And, as of a few months ago, I knew a thing or two about beings who were not of this earth.)

When the musical number ended, the audience rose to its feet, myself included, and burst into applause. Angela graciously took a bow and then performed several more songs before motioning for her company to join her at the front of the stage for a final bow. Then the house lights dimmed, and there was shuffling in the dark. When the stage lights came back on, Angela was alone, and the cheering continued as members of the audience pulled flowers from their table centerpieces and tossed them on stage.

Kurt Walker returned, clapping enthusiastically. "How wonderful!" he said. "May I say, Ms. Decatur, it has been a lifelong dream for me to see you in person, performing, and it was even more enchanting than I ever thought it could be. Thank you for this very special night. What a tremendous way to kick off our conference."

Angela smiled demurely but didn't say anything. If she hadn't just performed a series of songs, I would have wondered if she could talk at all. She took one last, long bow and began to make her way offstage. As she walked toward the balcony, her fellow dancers formed a line on both sides of her and cheered her on.

"She does private gigs now?" Jonah asked Sissy, his brows furrowing.

"I guess. Not sure, though," Sissy said.

"I wonder how much she got paid for this," Jonah asked.

"A pretty penny, I'd say," Stephanie said.

As the waiters returned to the room carrying trays of food, the dancers filtered in behind them, scattering across the room and talking with audience members. A man wearing a sailor's cap walked over to our table. He wasn't young—forties or fifties, maybe?—but he had the youthful exuberance of someone half his age.

"Hello, everyone! I hope you enjoyed the performance," he gushed as our waiter distributed dinner. "My name is Ted Matheson, and I'm proud to say I'm one of the dancers in Angela's wonderful residency next door."

"I enjoyed it very much," Sissy said. "So cohesive. Like you've all been performing together for years."

"Well, it's been about six months, but—between you and me—sometimes it *feels* like years." He gave one of those hearty laughs that usually follows a spit-take.

"I heard that the residency just got renewed for another year," Sissy said.

Ted nodded. "That's right. It's been very popular. We are very lucky."

As Ted continued talking, I began eating my salmon and looked around for Angela Decatur. I wanted to tell her how much I enjoyed her performance. But she wasn't at any of the tables. Then I saw her. She was outside on the balcony, alone, staring off at the Las Vegas skyline. Maybe she was too much of a veteran to do audience work. Or perhaps she needed the rest.

"How long have you been performing?" Stephanie asked Ted.

"Oh, gosh, since I was a little kid. My dad is the entertainment director for the Bellagio, right down the road, and he's been bringing me backstage ever since I could walk. I've met all the biggies."

"Are they as nice offstage as they are on stage?" Stephanie asked.

Ted put his hand to his lips and pretended to turn a key. "I've been sworn to secrecy," he said, and we laughed.

"Oh, you're no fun," Stephanie pouted.

"Well, you look like *you're* lots of fun!" he said, glancing at the three empty drink glasses in front of Stephanie, and we all laughed again.

Another performer came over, a woman with short blond hair that reminded me of my wig at home. She introduced herself as Carrie, and she and Ted began to regale us with stories of life on the stage when suddenly someone screamed.

I looked toward the balcony, where the noise came from. A waiter, the one who had taken my entrée order, was carrying an empty tray in one hand and, with the other, was reaching for a waitress who was sobbing uncontrollably. The waitress was pointing to the edge of the balcony.

People all around me stood up as the waiter put his tray down and pulled the waitress back. Tears streamed down her face, and she kept pointing at the ledge.

"She went over!" the waitress cried. "She jumped! I saw her!"

People in the room, including Declan, ran toward the scene as Kurt Walker appeared from the other end of the balcony, trying to usher the conference attendees back into the main ballroom, his face pale and concerned. He spoke quietly to the waiter consoling the waitress, and the waiter took out a phone and began to make a call.

"What's going on?" Stephanie whispered to me.

"I don't know."

Once the balcony was empty again, Kurt Walker put his dinner jacket over the shoulders of the waitress, and he and the waiter helped her off the balcony into the ballroom and then through one of the doors leading to the lobby.

"What happened?" someone shouted.

"Is that young woman all right?" called another.

As the audience began murmuring, Declan returned to his seat at our table, his face pale, his breathing a little heavy.

"What happened?" Stephanie asked.

He shook his head. "Angela Decatur."

"What about her?" Sissy asked.

Declan took a deep breath. "I think she jumped from the balcony. I think she's dead."

Chapter 6

JUMPED???

Oh no.

I couldn't stop picturing Angela Decatur standing on the balcony, looking out at all of Las Vegas, and thinking how maybe I could have been able to help if I had known she was troubled. I could have told her about the life I escaped in New York and the happy surprises I encountered in Salem. My new family. And that if I could change my life and overcome the odds, perhaps she could, too. But now I wouldn't have the chance.

Ugh. I thought I had developed a good sense about people, but there hadn't been anything in Angela Decatur's body language that told me something was wrong. She appeared pensive on the balcony, not suicidal. After all, she was a woman who had just performed an outstanding set to the roar of thunderous applause.

The police arrived shortly, causing even more confusion and fear among the conference attendees. They cordoned off the balcony area, and slowly, word began to spread about what had happened. Members of Angela Decatur's dance troupe were crying as were several members of the wait staff and audience.

"I'm afraid I have terrible news."

Kurt Walker was standing on the stage again, looking nothing like the man who had been fawning over Angela Decatur less than an hour ago. There were dark circles around his eyes. A sag to his stature. Her death had changed him. Changed us all.

"It appears Angela Decatur lost her life this evening," he said.

A few gasps sprang from the audience.

"I don't know what to say," Kurt said. "But I think it's important we keep the speculation to a minimum. And, please, no cell phones. We want to respect the gravity of the situation. We don't know for sure what's happened."

"She committed suicide!" a tall woman in the back shouted.

"I think she must have fallen!" called a man at the next table.

"Is the conference going to continue?!" another person asked.

"Please, everyone …" Kurt motioned with his hands for the audience to settle down. "As I said, we don't know what's happened. And we will let the authorities do their job. But I do want to say something …" He stood a little taller. "Angela Decatur will be greatly missed. She has meant a lot to audiences across the world. And to me personally." He took a deep breath and exhaled slowly. "As for the rest of the conference … Truly, one never knows how to proceed in a situation like this. And although some may view this as an indelicate choice, I believe for the good of our attendees, we will go on with the conference as scheduled. In doing so, I would like to think I was taking a page from the Angela Decatur handbook. She was once quoted as saying, 'We must do what compels us.'"

More murmuring in the audience. Kurt looked like he suddenly wanted to take back what he said as it seemed to create even more speculation. *Had Angela been compelled to jump to her death?* Eyes glistening from tears, Kurt looked over at the police officers near the balcony and along the perimeter of the large room. "I've been told that law enforcement would like to speak to each of us here to get a quick statement, and I implore you to cooperate and let them do their job. Obviously, the rest of this evening's engagements will be cut short." He pointed to the restaurant staff standing near the tables, holding pitchers of water. "The bartenders and waiters have kindly agreed to stay in case you need anything. Once you are cleared to go by the officers, you may leave. Those of you who do not wish to continue with the conference, I completely understand. Please reach out to me, and we will work something out. Otherwise, I will see you all here tomorrow morning for breakfast and we will try to carry on." He left the stage.

"I just can't believe it," Sissy said, picking up her purse from the back of her chair. "Committing suicide? There had been some talk about Angela Decatur needing throat surgery, but she sounded wonderful, didn't she?"

"Maybe she really did fall," I offered.

"From the top of a ledge?" Jonah asked, incredulous. "She would have had to climb up there." He pointed to his phone. "It says here that she may have been having some money problems."

"Before, when I was near the balcony, I overheard one of the dancers say she had been battling depression," Declan said.

"That happens sometimes with older female performers," Jonah said.

"*Excuse* me?" Stephanie said.

"Well, it's true." Jonah shrugged his big, husky shoulders. "As they get older, many female actresses are not able to get work."

"Newsflash, some of us are okay with getting older," Sissy said with an eyeroll.

"It's not *my* rule," Jonah said.

"Such a double standard," Stephanie muttered.

"But it sounded like Angela Decatur had a thriving residency," I said. "It was just renewed. Isn't that what that Ted guy said?"

"Listen, we can speculate on and on," Sissy said with a wave of her hand. "But Kurt Walker is right. The truth is, you just don't know what's going on in people's private lives."

Yep, that's for sure. I reached for the pitcher of water at the same time as Alice, and when our eyes met, she looked away.

"If Angela Decatur did this, it's clear she was suffering in some way," Sissy said. "May she rest in peace."

Police officers began visiting the tables in the room, interviewing the conference goers and writing on notepads.

"More water for the table, ma'am?"

Behind me, our table's waiter was holding a pitcher of ice water.

"Yes, thank you," I said.

As the waiter replaced the nearly empty pitcher with a fresh one, my eyes wandered to the far end of the room, where a police officer was chatting with Kurt Walker. Behind them, a single lone figure was watching.

A woman.

In a long, elegant dress.

All gray.

Angela Decatur's ghost.

Well, I guess that decided it. Angela Decatur had *not* fallen from the ledge. If she had, if her death had been accidental, her ghost wouldn't have remained behind. (I was learning *way* too much about the workings of the paranormal world.) Since it was here, she must have jumped. Committed suicide. Just like Beth Wyatt back in Salem, whose ghost was haunting the old Wyatt House.

I was about to pour myself some more water, proud of how I had solved the mystery of Angela Decatur's death, when I stopped.

Wait ...

Something wasn't making sense.

I stood up.

"Where are you going?" Stephanie asked.

"Um, I'm just going to get some seltzer from the bartender. Something bubbly to settle my stomach." I was hoping Stephanie remembered from our Wyatt House adventure that I sometimes had a nervous stomach. She seemed to, resuming her conversation with Jonah about the importance of representation of older women in Hollywood.

I walked toward the bartender, getting behind an older gentleman who was already in line. As I waited, I stared at Angela's figure. So sophisticated. Even in gray. I wanted to ask her how she got up here. That was the part that wasn't making sense. Ghosts appeared where they died. And by my calculations, if Angela Decatur committed suicide, then her ghost should be somewhere on Las Vegas Boulevard, wandering around near her dead body. Not here in this ballroom, twenty-seven stories up.

After I thanked the bartender for my seltzer, I turned and found myself looking directly into Angela Decatur's gray, hooded eyes, which were fixed upon me.

My breathing hitched.

My pulse raced.

Oh no. There was *another* reason why Angela Decatur's ghost was standing a few feet in front of me. And before I could scurry back to my group and forget I had ever come walking over here, she took a step toward me and in that deep, Tony-Award-winning dramatic voice said, "Can't these bumbling fools see that I was *murdered*?"

Chapter 7

I DIDN'T KNOW WHAT to do. Hurry back to my table and hide myself among the living? Down my water and fake a choking incident? (Let's face it: I wasn't that good of an actress.) Tell her I had reached my quota of murdered ghosts for the year?

"Idiots," Angela Decatur said, watching the police. "Just because a woman reaches a certain age doesn't mean she's ready to do away with herself at the first opportunity."

Take *that*, Jonah.

I turned my body so that my back was facing the tables in the room and held the glass to my mouth. "But people *are* saying that you were depressed," I said.

She glared at me. "My dear, people say all kinds of things. *Rarely* are they right." She crossed her arms. "Why is it you are the only person in this room who can see me and help me?"

That was the question of the year. And I had no answer. I took a quick sip of seltzer. If my stomach wasn't already nervous, it was now. "I can see you, but ... um, I can't help you."

"And why is that, my dear?"

"Because ..." *Yes, my dear, why can't you?* "I'm ... I'm here for the business conference." *Ugh. I definitely had to work at being quicker on my feet.*

"Well, bully for you."

"I'm setting up a bed-and-breakfast."

"A bed-and-breakfast, you say?" She rolled her gray eyes theatrically. "A bed-and-breakfast is not rocket science, my dear. Put out some clean towels and linens, and that's all you need to know. I've stayed in the most *dreadful* bed-and-breakfasts over the years. They'll call anything a luxury accommodation nowadays."

"I think there's more to it than that," I said a bit defensively. I glanced back at my table, where Stephanie was watching me, concerned. I think Alice was side-eye-watching, too, but it was difficult to tell. A police officer was finishing up with the table next to ours and began approaching Jonah.

"I have to go. Sorry. One of the officers is walking toward our table. And ... um ... well, good luck to you!" *Good luck to you?*

As I hurried back, I prayed Angela Decatur wasn't following me. With each step, I tried to convince myself she had simply decided there was no way a redheaded, seltzer-guzzling, aspiring bed-and-breakfast proprietor would be able to help her with her murder problem—even if she *was* the only one in the room who could see her.

It was a long shot, but I was betting on it.

No sooner had I sat down than I saw Angela Decatur following me. (Thank goodness I wasn't a gambler. My betting instincts stank.) Even in death, her steps were measured and methodical, not appearing to be in any rush, but she was zeroing in on me like a theater focal point.

"Miss?"

The police officer was standing beside me. *Has he been talking to me?* "Oh," I said. "I'm sorry, I'm not feeling well."

"She's a little shaken up," Stephanie said, reaching out to hold my arm. "She's got a bit of a nervous stomach."

"I think all of our stomachs are nervous after tonight," Declan said.

"I was just asking if you saw anything?" the officer said to me.

"Saw anything?" I sat there, unsure. Because if he was asking me if I *saw* something, the answer was a hard no. But if he was asking me if I *see* something—as in present tense, right now, in front of me—the answer was a resounding yes.

"Um, no. I didn't see anything ... *before.*" *Not a lie.*

Jotting something onto his notepad, the officer narrowed his blue eyes and studied me. He had every reason to. I was showing all the signs of deception. Nervousness. Hesitation. Fidgeting. Repeating questions. The list went on and on.

As he asked me for a spelling of my name—since, apparently, my conference badge wasn't good enough for him—I began spelling it out as Angela Decatur finally made it to the table. Boy, that long gown must have been heavy. Even for a ghost.

Angela stood behind Alice and glanced at everyone—Sissy, Declan, Stephanie, Jonah, the top of Alice's head—and then she read the placard at the top of the table centerpiece.

"Sa-lem Small Bus-i-ness Group," Angela said, enunciating every syllable and making the organization sound like a vocal exercise. "Are we all opening a bed-and-breakfast? Or are some of you actually hoping to make money?"

"Miss?"

The officer. He was talking to me again.

"Yes?" I said.

"Isn't your name Clara Kelly?" he asked. "That's the name on your badge."

"Yes."

"But the name you began spelling was A-N-G ..."

Ugh. I was spelling *Angela*. "Sorry. Like I said." I pointed to my head. "Not feeling great. My name is Clara Kelly. C-L-A R-A K-E-L-L-Y."

"Do you have any ID on you?" the officer asked, probably deciding he no longer felt comfortable trusting anything my badge—or *I*—said.

"No, not on me, I'm afraid. Other than this." I lifted the conference badge.

"Where on earth does he expect you to put identification?" Angela Decatur asked in a huff. "You're wearing a cocktail dress, for crying out loud." She sighed loudly and dramatically. "You know, I wore a dress just like that in a film I did back in the sixties titled *Far-out Flamingoes*. That was pre-varicose veins, of course. Later in my career, my legs had been insured for millions."

"Well, contact me if you think of anything, Ms. Kelly," the officer said, handing me a card. "My phone number is on there."

"Yes, thank you, officer."

As he circled the table toward Declan, Angela Decatur started saying my name.

"Clara, is it, my dear? Clara Kelly?"

Great. She heard my name. Was I going to have to change my name? *Again?* I reached for my glass of water since my seltzer was practically gone. Was it crazy to think I could just ignore her and focus on why I was here? To learn how to become a bed-and-breakfast entrepreneur? (That *was* why I was here, wasn't it?)

"Clara?" Angela Decatur said again.

I watched as the officer moved from Declan to Sissy, drinking my water, trying my best to drown out Angela's voice with the sound of my own swallowing. I couldn't understand how I continued to get myself into these predicaments. Why did I have to wander over to the corner of the room? Why couldn't I just sit here with the rest of the conference attendees in blissful ignorance? Curiosity, be damned!

I stopped drinking when I realized I no longer heard Angela. Had she gone? I didn't want to look in her direction, but I hoped she had gotten bored with me and decided to stare down someone else.

Suddenly, Angela's deep, gravelly voice burst into song—a raucous Broadway number I couldn't place, but whose unexpected ferocity startled me.

"Doooo I have yourrrrrr attention nowwww?!" Angela sang loudly as if she were trying to reach the audience at the back of a theater.

I sat there, stunned.

"What's the matter, Clara?" Stephanie asked. "Are you all right?"

"Ma'am?" the police officer asked, eyeing me curiously.

I couldn't catch my breath to answer either of them.

That's because when Angela suddenly belted out her Broadway tune, I wasn't the only one to startle.

I wasn't the only one who heard.

To my surprise, Alice did, too.

Chapter 8

Alice's and my eyes met for an instant.

"Are you all right, ma'am?" the officer asked again.

"Clara, maybe you should lie down." Stephanie reached for my arm.

"No, really, I'm okay," I said, nodding at the officer, who was handing Sissy his business card.

"Well, this table is cleared to go then," he said. "Remember, you all have my contact information. If you think of *anything*," he looked directly at me, "call me."

"Got it," I said and was about to stand when Alice was already up and hurrying toward the lobby.

"Wait, Alice!" I called.

But she didn't stop. I grabbed my purse and followed behind.

At the elevators, people were milling around, talking in hushed tones, and Alice glided past them to the back and then ducked into a bathroom. I tried to follow her when I heard Stephanie call my name.

"What's going on with Alice? Are the two of you all right?" she said when she caught up to me.

"I'm fine. Really. I just need a minute. I'm sure Alice is fine, too. I'll see you in the morning for breakfast."

"Maybe I should wait for you."

"Don't be silly." I smiled as if there was nothing to worry about, as if a murdered ghost hadn't driven at least one member of the Salem Small Business Group into a public bathroom to hide. "All is well. I'm excited to move forward tomorrow with business learning." *Business learning?*

"Okay, but just know that it's all right if you and Alice are freaked out," Stephanie said. "It's going to be hard to put tonight behind us." She shook her head. "That poor woman. I'm here if you need me. See you tomorrow, Clara."

"See you tomorrow!" I chirped.

I watched Stephanie get into the elevator and then ran straight for the bathroom.

When I got inside, it was empty. All the stall doors were open.

Except one.

"Alice, I know you're in here."

Silence.

I didn't want to check under the stalls for feet like in a horror film, so I decided to just stand where I was, blocking the exit. There was no other way out, so Alice would have to come this way. Unless she decided to pull a Nemo and follow the pipe water to the ocean. "Alice, please."

Silence.

I didn't know how long I was standing there, but the chatter outside quieted down. Maybe an elevator had arrived. Maybe more than one. Finally, a toilet flushed, sending a shock of sound through the tiled bathroom, and Alice stepped directly to the sinks without looking at me.

"Alice ..."

She continued washing her hands.

"Alice, you heard her, didn't you?"

Alice reached for a paper towel. "I have to go," she said quietly, pushing her glasses up the bridge of her nose.

"But, wait ..." I stepped in front of her. "I need to talk to you, please. I know you—"

Suddenly, Alice zigged as I zagged, and she got around me and left the bathroom. For a quiet and reserved gal, she was surprisingly slippery.

"Wait!" I tried to follow her but wound up slamming into two older women walking into the bathroom.

"Excuse you, young lady," one of them said, brushing off the front of her dress like I had dropped cookie crumbs onto it.

"Sorry," I said. "Excuse me."

When I got to the lobby, Alice wasn't there, but an elevator door was just about to close. If I hurried, I could make it. Before I could try, though, Angela Decatur waltzed in front of me, arms extended, taking up space.

"I seeeee I've finallyyyy gotten your attentionnnn," she sang.

I should have just walked through her.

I knew I could.

But somehow that seemed ... impolite?

Instead, I watched the elevator doors close. With Alice inside the elevator. And not me.

"My dear, if you must know, I would very much prefer to have one of the Keystone cops back there help me in my current predicament," Angela Decatur said, "but, as we established, you are the only one who can see and hear me."

Not true. At least, I didn't think so. But I needed to talk to Alice first. "I'm sorry," I said. "I need to go."

"Go?!" she asked, bewildered. "You always seem to be on the go. Here. There. Back and forth. And yet you never seem to arrive anywhere. Like a rocking chair. Have you noticed?"

"Listen," I said, lowering my voice when two men entered the lobby. "I know this is disorienting for you. And I'm so sorry for that." My phone began vibrating in my purse, followed by the strains of classical music. A text from William. Geez, there were ghosts everywhere. "And I know you feel like I'm the only one who can help you. And I feel for you." More buzzing from my purse. More classical music. Another text from William? Possibly another photo of Ghost Cat that didn't feature Ghost Cat? "But I just can't do this right now."

"I understand how you feel," Angela said.

"You do?" I asked, relieved.

"Yes, of course. When I played Laurie Hellman, an author in the play *Write or Wrong*, she had a similar dilemma to make. And unlike you, as much as it hurt her, she chose the less selfish one."

"Did you say *selfish*?"

"Sometimes by helping others, we help ourselves, my dear." She raised her hands, as if reciting a monologue to the gods above. "I said so in my acceptance speech that year when I won Best Actress for playing Laurie Hellman."

"I'm sorry. I'm not familiar with the play or the speech."

"No? The speech made quite a splash, you know. It was on all the evening newscasts."

"That's great, but, listen, I really have to go. And there really is a good chance *someone* at the conference can help you." I wasn't naming names. I wasn't a squealer. But if I knew children could see ghosts, and possibly Alice could, too, then that meant I wasn't the *only* adult on Planet Earth who could. And this conference had adults attending from across the globe. The odds were good that *someone somewhere* would be able to help Angela Decatur find her murderer. (Although, as already established, my gambling instincts were not on point.)

"My dear, I don't believe there is anyone else who can help me," Angela said. "I've walked the entire length of the ballroom several times, and no one has noticed me. It is *ghastly*." (Did she mean *ghostly*? Not important.)

"For years, I had wished for such a thing," Angela continued. "To be able to go to the grocery store and not be besieged by autograph seekers. And now when I finally don't attract attention, I need it." She sighed. "Another irony of life." (Did she mean *afterlife*? Again, not important.)

"I have to go, Ms. Decatur."

"Fine. Go. Hop into your rocking chair," she said. "You may call me Angela, by the way, my dear. Even though you haven't earned it. Yes, I know it's very magnanimous of me."

Gee, thanks. "Okay. Well, then, I guess ..."

"Good luck?" Angela asked sarcastically.

"Um, I guess. I'm sorry. Goodbye."

As I ran toward the elevators, I could feel Angela watching as I jammed my finger on the down button. Miraculously, a pair of elevator doors opened right near me, and I leaped inside the elevator. When I turned around, Angela was still staring at me.

She continued to stare (and stare) until the doors took their (very) sweet time closing.

Like the final curtain of a play.

Only I had a feeling this play was going to have one more act.

And with a possible murderer lurking around, I hoped it wasn't a cliffhanger.

Literally.

Chapter 9

"Are you all right, Clara?" Stephanie asked, reaching for the coffeepot.

No, I was *not* all right. I was exhausted. And ornery. And I probably had BO since I had overslept and didn't have time to shower. Just the right frame of mind to begin my very first business conference.

"I was hoping to talk to Alice," I said, pouring myself two cups of coffee. With any luck, I'd be able to scarf down a third. "Have you seen her?"

"Didn't you see her last night in the bathroom?" Stephanie asked.

Ugh. That's right. The last thing Stephanie knew was that I was running to the bathroom behind Alice. "No, I didn't. Unfortunately. Long story." I put my hand on my stomach.

"Oh, I hope you're feeling better," Stephanie said. "Alice texted me this morning. She isn't feeling well either and said she was going to skip this morning's sessions. You know, come to think of it, Alice *also* had the salmon. Do you think the two of you had food poisoning?"

I'm pretty sure that isn't what's bothering Alice. "Maybe?" I offered.

"Well, I asked if there was anything I could do, but she said she was fine and would attend the sessions virtually and meet up with the group later." Stephanie reached for a jelly donut. "Thank goodness Alice isn't here to see these donuts—if you can call them donuts. The Haunted Cookie's stuff is so much better." She grabbed a napkin.

Great. I had scared Alice away. It probably hadn't been a good idea to knock on her hotel room door last night, again and again, hoping she might talk to me. I would have knocked even more if I hadn't been worried someone—possibly Alice—would call security on me.

"How did you sleep?" Stephanie reached for a bottle of apple juice.

"Okay," I said, although I spent most of the night wide awake, wondering what it meant that Alice could see ghosts. Would we finally have something to talk about?

"I'll get us a table," Stephanie said.

I grabbed a bagel and slathered it with enough cream cheese to frost a cake, adding it to my tray. Then I adjusted the strap of my briefcase and walked into the main room.

All the tables were still set up from the night before, new flowers in the centerpieces, which were flanked by the morning newspapers and complimentary legal pads and pens stamped with the conference logo. So much for bringing my own pads and pens.

Stephanie selected a table at the far end of the room, and as I neared it, I could see Angela standing off to the side, her long gray dress flowing behind her.

Unsurprisingly, she was staring directly at me.

I averted my eyes and tried not to think about her roaming these halls all night long. Alone. Not able to leave because she didn't know how to manipulate physical objects. Not able to ask for help because no one could see or hear her. Not able to find her murderer because *selfish* Clara Kelly had enough on her mind.

"Clara, over here!" Stephanie called.

By the time I got to the table, Sissy and Declan were seated beside Stephanie.

"Well, it looks like most people stayed for the conference," Sissy said, looking around.

"You can't really blame them," Declan said. "Between the conference fee and the travel expenses, this was a lot to invest."

I bit into my bagel and glanced at Angela, who had moved over to the closed-off balcony area, gazing out at the Las Vegas skyline as she had the night before when she was still alive.

The table got quiet, and I realized Sissy, Declan, and Stephanie were studying the conference schedule.

"What are you attending, Clara?" Stephanie asked. "I think I'm going to sit in on the panel called How to Hire the Right Person."

"I was thinking of that one as well," Declan said.

I smiled. I had a feeling Declan would be attending whatever panel Stephanie was. And I was happy he chimed in to answer because, somehow, with all the time I had last night staring at the ceiling, I had neglected to look over the morning's panel schedule.

"Good people are hard to find," Stephanie said. "Being a tour guide isn't really suited to every personality. I need workers who are not only comfortable with people but who like the historical aspect of the job. They memorize a lot of facts. The good ones do, anyway." She took a bite of her donut. "And then there's the performance aspect of it. That's a lot of pressure. A tour guide can make or break a person's vacation."

"Sold," Sissy said. "Maybe I'll attend that one as well. We're thinking about extending our business hours at Haute Chocolate and will be hiring a few new people."

Stephanie stuck the rest of her donut into her mouth and grabbed her coffee, juice, and other things. "We'd better go now if we're going to get good seats."

"I'm right behind you." Declan pushed out his chair.

"Will you be joining us, Clara?" Sissy asked, standing.

"I don't think I'm ready to hire anyone yet," I said. "I was hoping to try a panel that was a little more ... basic."

"Okay, we'll see you at lunch then," Stephanie said. "Have a good morning!"

"You too!" I said, watching them go and suddenly feeling alone.

And vulnerable.

Angela was still standing over by the balcony, but she might be enticed to come over with everyone gone. I quickly looked over the conference materials. The faster I could find a panel to attend, the faster I could leave the ballroom. There was a session on "Learning to Say No." I glanced at Angela. That might be a good one. Not only for negotiating in business, but for what apparently had become my side hustle: negotiating with murdered ghosts. I couldn't dodge Angela forever. Or keep coming up with excuses. Or running off. I had done enough running.

"Is this seat taken?"

Glenn Swanson, the guy who struck up a conversation with me last night, was standing over me, wearing a powder blue button-down shirt and tan trousers. A laptop sleeve was under his arm, a cup of coffee in his hand.

"No, not at all," I said, grateful to have another body at my table—one that was living and breathing.

He sat down and placed his items in front of him. "That was crazy stuff last night, huh?" he said.

You have no idea. "Yeah, I know."

"I was surprised they decided to go on with the conference." He took a long sip of his coffee. "Kind of insensitive, don't you think?"

I shrugged. "It's hard to say. I try not to judge people. I feel most people just try to make the best decision they can at the time." At least that's what I told myself after marrying Joe.

"That's very mature of you." Glenn stared into my eyes, searching. "So, what panel are you attending this morning?"

"Not sure yet."

"Anything seem interesting?" His eyes were still searching mine.

"Well, I was thinking about this *no* panel." I pointed to the page in front of me.

He winked. "Well, if you ask me, saying no is overrated." And suddenly his hand was on mine.

I pulled my hand back. "I'm sorry?"

Glenn chuckled. "Why do you look so surprised? We had a moment last night, didn't we?"

"We did?"

"Yeah, at the cocktail party. I saw the way you were looking at me."

How *I* was looking at *him*? "I think you were mistaken. I was looking at you like a person I just met at a cocktail party."

"*Please ...*" He laughed again.

I knew that laugh. Joe used to laugh like that. When he was gaslighting me. When he wanted to make it seem like I didn't know what I was doing or what I was talking about.

"Well," he said. "You know how these Vegas conferences are. People can have a little vay-cay from their significant others and, well, have a little fun. I thought you might want to—"

"Well, you thought wrong." I put my agenda into my briefcase and packed up my stuff.

"Why?" he asked. "Got a boyfriend you're staying true to?"

Why was it some men thought you needed to have a boyfriend to say no to them? "No, I don't have a boyfriend. I'm just not interested."

Glenn looked shocked. Like a woman had never said no to him before. But that's all he was going to get from me. A hard no. I laughed inside. *I guess I don't need the Learn How to Say No panel, after all.*

Then Glenn's look of shock turned to something else. Embarrassment? Anger? I was getting a weird vibe. He began looking at me the way Joe used to. Like a predator. The only difference was Joe never showed that side of him out in public. He hid it behind closed doors. Glenn either didn't care or wasn't as good at duplicity.

"You don't know what you're missing out on," he said as I stood up. "I know how to treat a woman." He folded his arms, revealing a Rolex watch on his wrist and a ring on his finger that probably cost more than my car.

Suddenly, something that cynical Uber driver said came to mind.

Don't be distracted by the shiny penny.

My mind began putting images and ideas together. Angela standing on the balcony. Finding out there was a murderer possibly roaming around the conference. Glenn Swanson hitting on me and reluctant to take no for an answer. An undercurrent of anger. The similarities to Joe, who had a propensity for violence. I placed my briefcase strap on my shoulder. "By the way, where were you when it happened?" I blurted.

Glenn seemed taken aback. "Where was I when what happened?"

"You know, when Angela Decatur ..." I pointed to the balcony.

"I wasn't here," he said.

"You left the cocktail reception?"

"If you must know, I stepped outside into the lobby to make a call." The left corner of his mouth twitched.

He's lying.

My heart began beating faster, and there was a *whooshing* in my ears. Why was Glenn Swanson lying about where he was when Angela had been murdered?

One big reason came to mind. *Because he is the murderer.*

"Why do you ask?" he said, also standing.

Play it cool. I casually shrugged. (Well, I hoped it was casually.) "I just don't remember seeing you."

He smiled. "Why, were you looking for me?"

"No, I wasn't."

"*Sure*, you weren't." His smile tightened. "Well," he whispered, "between you and me, you don't know what you're missing. But I hope you find something to do this morning that interests you."

I realized right then that I *had* decided which panel I was going to attend. Any panel that Glenn Swanson *wasn't*.

Glenn pulled down his expensive shirt sleeves and strode toward the conference rooms, leaving his unfinished coffee on the table.

Sebastian had made a comment about the possibility of my making friends while I was in Las Vegas. That remained to be seen. (And whether one of those friends would be Alice was another big question mark.) But judging by my interaction with Glenn Swanson, it looked like I might have just made my first enemy.

Chapter 10

THE MORNING *DRAAAAGGGGGED*. ALL I could think about during the session I decided to attend, Understanding the Basics of Small Business, was that I needed to talk to Alice. And, finally, when that session was over and I decided to stand by the elevator so I could ambush her as she came to the twenty-seventh floor to eat (she couldn't pass up an already-paid-for lunch, could she?), she never showed. (Apparently, she could.)

I eventually got in the lunch buffet line before time ran out. Glenn Swanson spotted me and ran off in the other direction like I had the plague. (For those keeping count, that was *two* individuals—Alice and Glenn—who were avoiding *me* and *one*—Angela—*I* was avoiding. No wonder I was having trouble concentrating.)

I found myself sliding onto a table next to Jonah and Sissy, trying to make small talk. They were nearly finished with their lunch, and before I knew it, they were up and heading to the next session.

For the first of two afternoon sessions, I had chosen a panel discussion about Leveraging the Power of Social Media and was determined to learn something. *Anything.* I quickly finished my lunch, found the location of the session, took my things to the front of the room, Stephanie-style, opened my laptop, and tried to clear my mind.

The room filled up quickly. It wasn't a secret that social media marketing was crucial to a business. Not only could you engage with large numbers of clients and customers simultaneously, but you could do it practically for free. Count me in! Even though I had inherited quite a bit of money from Joe, I needed to learn to run my business effectively and efficiently. Especially since my ex-sister-in-law was trying to take all my inheritance away from me. A shoestring budget was very possibly in my future.

Just as the first panelist, a woman who owned a home health aide staffing company, was finishing up her overview of the various social media sites she used, as well as their pros and cons—

Bang!

Something fell at the back of the room.

I turned, as did most of the audience, and saw that one of the waiters had apparently dropped a coffee pot. Another waiter—the one who had been serving us last night—rushed over to help. I suddenly thought of the young waitress on the balcony he had also helped, the one who had seen Angela *jump*.

Had she really seen her jump? How could that be when Angela said she had been murdered? Had the waitress been lying? *Acting?*

I erased the questions from my mind. This was not my problem. Social media marketing was my problem. A big one. And I was here to find answers.

As I turned back in my seat, my eyes swept across the attendees, and that's when I saw her.

Alice.

Sitting at a table way in the back.

She glanced at me, and I could see her grip her notepad, ready to duck out the door if she saw me coming. It took every ounce of strength I had to concentrate on the rest of the presentation. *Remember why you're here …*

One of the panelists was talking about creating engaging video content and the importance of putting ourselves out there, how we were the best advocates for our business. Ugh. I'd have to get over my on-screen anxiety. I would have been happy to let William star in Kensington House Bed-and-Breakfast's social media reels if only he showed up in photography.

When the presentation was over, I slammed my laptop closed and grabbed my purse, hoping to catch Alice before she left, but, unsurprisingly, she was already gone. And I wasn't sure what panel she would be attending next. Most likely, it wasn't going to be the one *I* was heading to: hospitality marketing.

Outside the conference room, people were grabbing water bottles and hanging out at high-top tables and sitting on couches.

"Hey, lady!" Stephanie said, grabbing my arm. "Where you heading?"

"Hospitality marketing," I said.

"Sounds perfect for you."

"Yeah. One of the panel speakers, Stanley Paulson, was a visiting professor when I was in college. He was only a few years older than me but had already made a name for himself in the tourism field by opening a chain of book-themed hotels."

"Oh, that sounds even *more* perfect for you."

I just hoped I could concentrate enough to get something out of it. And not think about Angela or Alice or Glenn Swanson, who was possibly a murderer. (Although during lunch, he had run away from me like *I* was the murderer.) "I'd better go—you know, if I'm going to get a seat in the *front row*." I winked.

"Atta girl! Front rows rule! See you later, Clara."

I hurried into the conference room and nabbed the last front-row seat. I scanned the panelists who were seated and spotted Stanley Paulson immediately. He was the youngest person on the panel—by far. He must have been in his mid-thirties, but he had a boyish look about him with a mop of dark brown hair and round cheeks. He hadn't changed all that much since I had seen him in college.

The panel turned out to be fascinating, and I was typing as quickly as I could to get all the nuggets of information down. The part I found most relevant was about promoting safety—making sure I highlighted safety procedures and Kensington House's hygiene policies when guests arrived. *Looks like I'll be investing in a lot of disinfectant.*

I thought of Cindy and Wayne, the couple I had managed to talk into staying at Kensington House for a hundred bucks when I first arrived. How much dust there had been in the house! Hopefully, future guests of the bed-and-breakfast wouldn't need to bring their own can of Pledge.

When the discussion was over, I waited patiently for Stanley Paulson to shake hands with the other members of the panel before I approached. When he spotted me, he smiled warmly.

"I just wanted to say how much I enjoyed your comments today," I said, getting a little flustered. I wasn't sure why, although I always did get nervous when I had to speak with a teacher or a professor. "We've met before. At SUNY Binghamton."

"Thank you." He looked at my badge. "Clara Kelly. I don't remember the name."

You wouldn't, considering that wasn't my name then.
"Well, it was a long time ago."

"Kensington House Bed-and-Breakfast, huh? In Salem? Sounds like a great place to open a B&B."

"I hope so. I'm supposed to be opening in a few months."

"Well, you're in the right place. The people who run this conference really are top-notch. It's a shame what happened last night. I feel like it's cast a gloomy pall on the whole thing. But it looks like a good number of people stayed."

"They probably need as much help as I do."

"Hey, you're attending the conference, which means you're putting effort into learning. And that will take you very far." He smiled again.

"Mr. Paulson!"

A pair of women were fangirling behind me, eager to get his attention.

"Well, I just wanted to say hi," I said. "Looks like you've got a few fans."

"I've got another panel tomorrow if you have any questions. I don't usually like spending the night in Las Vegas. I'm more of a small town, East Coast guy who doesn't really like the bright lights."

"Same."

"But one of the speakers bailed after last night," he said, "and they asked if I would fill in."

"That was nice of you to do it at the last minute."

"Couldn't say no. Kurt Walker's a cool guy. And a big supporter of mine."

"Okay, well, maybe I'll come back tomorrow, then." *Why would I come back tomorrow?* Did I have more questions? Or was it because Stanley Paulson was kinda cute, and he radiated warmth and kindness, and I didn't have much experience with those kinds of men? Other than my dad, of course. And Sebastian. And William. (Although I often had to wear a sweater when I was near William.) Ugh. I needed less focus on cute and more on commerce. *Be professional.*

As I walked away and the two girls began twittering about how they were "big fans," my phone pinged from my briefcase. I pulled it out. A text from Sebastian. How weird—I had been just thinking about him.

I clicked on the text, and staring back at me with his big eyes was Boy. Sebastian had groomed him again, and he looked adorable with his new haircut and fresh bowtie clip. I read Sebastian's text:

Everything all right here. No need to worry.

Before I could respond, Stephanie whispered into my ear, "So, who was that cute guy you were talking to? Is that the *professor* you were talking about? And here I was imagining some old guy who looked like Albert Einstein."

I laughed. "I told you he was only a few years older than me, silly."

"Well, let me tell you, the way he was looking at you looked like he wanted to talk about more than just shop."

Soooo not true. Or was it? *Be professional!*

"You've got a lot of eyes on you at this conference, Clara Kelly."

Stanley Paulson aside, she had no idea. A pair of gray eyes was probably gazing at me right now. And as the ballroom began emptying out as the last panels of the day concluded, sure enough, I could see Angela standing over by the balcony again—looking right at me. Had she been there all day? The guilt squeezed me like a coat that was too tight.

"Well, I think I need a shower before dinner," Stephanie said. "I'll see you later. We're not planning for dinner until around eight o'clock, so that will give you plenty of time to call your *friend* William?" She nudged me with her elbow.

I laughed. "Maybe." It wasn't a bad idea.

"I'll text you later and give you definitive plans. We're thinking about that 1950s diner place downstairs."

"Okay."

"See you, Clara Kelly! I have a date with a bar of soap!" Stephanie said, rushing off.

A shower was a good idea since I had skipped one this morning, but it wasn't the first thing on my mind. My main focus at the moment was to 1) get out of here before Angela Decatur made me feel any guiltier, and 2) track down Alice Sutton.

Chapter 11

I KNOCKED ON ALICE'S hotel door lightly. What I really wanted to do was slam my hand against it frantically, but I had decided in the elevator that would be the wrong course of action. I needed to handle Alice like I would a delicate flower, and considering I had a black thumb, this was going to be challenging.

Since last night, I had been wondering if I had seen what I thought I saw, and I was pretty sure I had—Alice jumped when Angela Decatur began to sing. Which meant that Alice heard her. Actually *heard* her. But I needed to talk to Alice to be sure.

I stood outside the door, waiting. Just like last night, but I couldn't imagine where else Alice could be. She *had* to be in there. I didn't take her for a gambler. And she cringed during nearly every social outing. I put my ear to the door, wondering if I would be able to hear a television, but there was no sound. I glanced down the long hotel hallway, which seemed scary without anyone coming or going; I expected Stephen King's *Shining* twins to appear and ask me to play with them. I knocked again, a little more frantically.

Nothing.

"Alice, please. We need to talk about this. Please open the door."

I waited some more. And some more. And just when I was about to turn around and return to my hotel room, with my ghost-whispering tail between my legs, I heard a noise behind Alice's door.

"Alice, is that you? Are you there?"

I looked at the door's tiny peephole, which went from light to dark. *She's looking through it.*

"Alice, please open the door. Let's talk."

Then, to my utter delight—and also shock—a tiny voice said through the door, "Are you alone?"

"Yes. Stephanie is in her room."

Silence. *Is that the wrong answer?*

"That's not what I mean," she said.

My eyes opened wide. She was referring to Angela Decatur. She must have been. My pulse quickened. Alice *had* heard her. And had probably seen her, too. "Yes, I'm alone."

After a painstakingly long moment, the deadbolt unlocked, and the door opened a tiny bit, the security chain hanging just below Alice's head. She peeked out at me.

"You can trust me, Alice. I promise."

Her eyes met mine, but the door closed once again, and I thought it might never open. But then I heard the chain slide, and the door opened with Alice standing behind it.

"May I come in?" I asked. She was wearing pink plaid pajamas that reminded me of some of the pretty cupcakes sold by The Haunted Cookie.

She shrugged. "Okay," she said in her tiny voice.

I hurried in before Alice changed her mind, and she closed the door quickly, as if expecting someone—or something—to follow behind me.

I didn't leave any time for an uncomfortable silence. "I'm sorry about what happened last night," I blurted. "I didn't mean to, um ... get so excited."

Alice walked past me and sat on a chair by the desk. She neatened some stacks of papers that looked like a script of some kind, but I didn't want to be nosy. *Well, nosier than I'm already being.*

"I really don't want to talk about what happened," she said.

"Can I just ask you something?"

She looked at me.

"Did you hear what I thought you heard? And see what I thought you saw?" I knew I was sounding like Dr. Seuss, but I was hoping the Sam I Am approach would seem less like an interrogation.

Alice let go of the papers she had been neatening. She took in a big breath and let it out slowly. She looked as though she was about to say something but changed her mind. "I can't," she said finally.

"May I sit?" I asked, pointing to one of the full-size beds. She nodded.

"You don't have to explain anything. Maybe *I'm* the one who does." Now, it was *my* turn to take a deep breath. When I let it out, I said, "I'm going to tell you something that nobody knows."

She looked up at me quickly, as if interested, but then her eyes returned to the paperwork.

"When I moved into Kensington House," I began, "I discovered that it was ... well, haunted."

Alice didn't say anything. She played with the staple at the top corner of one of the collated pages in front of her.

"I couldn't believe it," I said. "A ghost by the name of William Kensington was living there. He's from the eighteen hundreds. And I found myself talking to him. After the initial shock of it all, I became unafraid. William is kind. And, as strange as it sounds, he has become my friend. It was only a few hours after I first saw him that I realized I was the only one who could see him. No one else could see ghosts. Except for a few children. No one else ... but you."

Alice stopped fingering the staple.

"Yesterday, after the ... well, after Angela Decatur's death ... I saw her ghost. She told me she hadn't jumped. She told me she was *murdered*." I didn't know what kind of reaction I expected from Alice when I said that. Or maybe I did—*none*—and that was exactly the reaction I got. Meanwhile, *I* couldn't believe the words coming out of my mouth. A ghost told me she had been murdered? This was the first time I'd said these words out loud to anyone. I sounded crazy to myself. Would Alice think I was crazy? "Please tell me you believe me."

We sat there, still, for what seemed like a very long time, until Alice cleared her throat.

"I saw you," she said quietly.

"You saw me when?"

"At The Haunted Cookie. Back in March. You were with ... with ..."

My heart began pumping wildly.

Alice swallowed, like there was some obstruction that was keeping the words from coming out. "You were with Beckett."

A gasp slipped out of my mouth, and my hand flew to my face to stop it. "You *saw* Beckett's ghost?"

She gave a tiny, almost imperceptible nod.

"But you didn't. I was *sure* you didn't. I watched you. You looked at me and then went about the business of getting me my Fluffernutter—which was delicious, by the way—like Beckett's ghost wasn't even there. But you saw him the whole time?"

She nodded again. "And heard him."

"Wow." This was way too much information to absorb. Alice deserved an Academy Award for her performance. Angela Decatur had nothing on her. "Does that mean you saw Marlena Ryder's ghost, too, at Ye Olde Salem Book Shoppe? And Kai Teller's when we were at Wyatt House?"

She nodded, and I had the urge to leap into the air and kick my heels together in a leprechaun jump. "Oh, my gosh. I thought I was the only adult who could. And now here you are. Now there's someone I can talk to about all this."

Alice's eyes left me, and she straightened the paperwork again. "I don't want to talk about it."

"But why?"

"I don't want to see them. I don't want to hear them."

"Alice, I don't think it's something we can control. It just ... well, it just *is*."

"Not for me."

"Why not?"

Silence again.

"Please talk to me, Alice. I'm a friend. Well, I want to be. I'm a person you can trust."

Alice looked torn, like she wanted to talk but also was afraid to. I knew that feeling well. I had it every time I was at a social gathering with Joe, and he walked away for a moment. I wondered, *Can I confide in this person?* Could I tell them Joe was an abuser? Would he or she be able to help me? And then I would think of my father, and of my need to keep him safe, and I wound up never saying a word.

"How about I tell you something not many people know? Do you want to hear it?"

She shrugged. "Haven't you already?"

"I mean, besides the ghost thing."

Alice shrugged again.

"Well ..." My belly seized with anxiety. I hadn't really told anyone this. Besides William. "My real name is not Clara Kelly. It's Emily Turner. But I wanted a fresh start when I came to Salem. I wanted to leave behind who I was. So, I started with a new name."

Alice picked up a paperclip and began playing with it. "Sometimes I wish I could just change my name and go someplace else, too."

"Yeah, well, running away isn't usually the right answer."

"Then why did *you* do it?"

I shrugged. "Let's just say, it was a matter of life and death. Mine. My husband wasn't very nice."

Alice's eyes opened wide.

"He slapped me around a lot, and I worried that he might hurt my father," I said. "My father died earlier this year ..."

"I'm sorry."

"Thank you, but that was my chance to get away. I had planned it for a long time. I came to Salem, but I didn't do a good job of covering my tracks, and Joe ... well, he found me. And he wasn't too happy with me. But he ended up having an accident. He tripped over ... well, he tripped down the stairs and broke his neck." I closed my eyes remembering that day. "He can't hurt me anymore. And I decided to stay in Salem and start a new life. And to start a new business, which is why I'm here in Las Vegas."

Alice removed her hands from the paperwork and placed them in her lap. "It sounds like you've been through a lot."

"It sounds like we both have."

Alice wrapped her arms around herself like she was cold and looked down at the floor. "I started seeing them when I was a little girl." She was whispering like someone might hear her, besides me.

I exhaled. "Ghosts?"

She nodded. "When did *you* start seeing them?"

"William was my first," I said. "Back in March."

"I didn't know what they were. I knew they weren't like people. They were different. All gray. And I realized fast that no one else could see them but me. I would point them out to my mother when we went to the grocery store. There's lots of them in Salem."

I didn't say anything. I didn't want Alice to stop talking.

"When I showed them any kind of attention—eye contact or anything—they liked it. It was like they were waiting for someone to notice them." She paused, as if lost in the memory. "The problem was, they wouldn't leave me alone. They would talk to me nonstop—so much that I couldn't hear my mother at the playground when she was telling me it was time to come home. Or if she was asking me what I wanted for dinner. She thought I was ignoring her." She reached up and tightened the pink ponytail holder at the back of her head. "They started telling me that something had happened to them and they needed help. They just kept talking and talking, and then they would follow me to my house, and I was so afraid they would come in, but then I realized they couldn't come in. My house was safe."

"You have to invite them in," I said. "I learned that, too."

"I started not wanting to leave my house. I started not playing outside anymore. I became a totally different child. My mom thought there was something wrong with me. I just preferred to stay inside and read or watch TV. It was like that for a long time. Then, when I turned sixteen, she made me start working at The Haunted Cookie. And there was no getting out of that, so I had to figure out how to face these ghosts."

"What did you decide?"

"I decided I would not look at them. Or acknowledge them. Or listen to them. I would just teach myself to look past them, look through them, ignore them, so they wouldn't know I could see and hear them." She nodded. "So, that's what I did. And I got really good at it, too. So good that some of the ghosts who knew I could see them as a child thought I couldn't see them anymore. That I had grown out of the ability somehow. When I realized I could trick them, I started going out of the house more—to my mother's delight. I even started dating."

"You dated Beckett, right? He mentioned that."

"Yeah, he was kind of a jerk."

"Yeah," I said. "He kind of was."

Alice's eyes met mine, and we both smiled a little.

"But seeing ghosts changed me," she said. "I still don't like being around people much. I'm too self-conscious. I had wanted to go away to college, but I was too nervous that something might happen, that I might run into ghosts haunting the campus or whatever, so I ended up staying home and commuting to UMass Boston."

Alice had been kept from doing the things she wanted to do. Like me, Alice had been living in a prison. But this was a prison she had built herself.

"Sometimes, I slip," she said. "Like what happened upstairs last night. If a ghost managed to startle me or if, somehow, I made eye contact, they would get so excited. But I would get angry. At myself. At them for making me hide who I am."

Could that have been why Beckett thought Alice had an anger-management problem? Because she would get upset with herself sometimes? "Angela Decatur doesn't know you can see her," I said. "She was so focused on me that she didn't see you startle when she sang."

"It doesn't matter." Suddenly, Alice stood up. "I don't know why I said any of that."

"Maybe you needed to," I said, standing up with her. "Does it feel good to unload some of that?"

"I don't know."

"Listen, Alice, I know exactly how you feel. I didn't want to acknowledge them either. Or help them."

"Then why did you? You helped Beckett. And Marlena Ryder. And Kai Teller. I saw you help them all."

"I didn't want to help them at first," I said.

"Why did you change your mind?"

That was a good question. Why did I? I could have argued that Beckett Miller had tricked me into helping him. And that William had guilted me into helping Marlena. And that I didn't want to see Kai's charity lose the money it was entitled to. But I suddenly realized that wasn't the truth.

"I think, deep down inside, I *wanted* to help. I knew what it was like to feel trapped. And if I can help someone not feel that way, then I'm going to do it." I thought of Angela upstairs, probably gazing out the balcony window, alone, and the belt of my guilt-coat began to tighten again.

"I just can't help them," Alice said, looking at the floor. "I can't."

"That's okay. You don't have to."

"And you don't have to, either."

"I know." I nodded. "You're absolutely right. But, as I talk to you, I'm realizing that I kind of want to." I had wanted to start living my life authentically when I moved to Salem, and yet somehow it took a trip to Las Vegas—a fake city, according to my Uber driver—to get to my real truth. "Does that make me weird?"

Alice cracked a small smile again. "*All* of this is weird."

"That's for sure."

We stood there. Me looking at Alice. Alice looking at the bedspread. Which was closer to my eyes than the floor, so I considered that progress.

"I'd better go," I said finally.

"Okay," Alice said.

As I began walking toward the door, I stopped. "Oh, I think some of us might be getting together for dinner, if you'd like to join us."

"I think I might just stay here tonight."

"Okay. Well, if you change your mind, just let me know."

As I left Alice's hotel room and the door gently shut behind me, I listened to hear if Alice secured the deadbolt. She didn't.

More progress.

I took out my hotel room key so that I could go inside my room and shower off this long day, but I found myself walking, instead, toward the elevator bank.

There was someone else I needed to talk to tonight.

This time, on the twenty-seventh floor.

Chapter 12

When the elevator doors opened, the sound of vacuum cleaners greeted me. The ballroom was empty and seemed so much larger and cavernous than it did during the day. Cleaning crews were at the far end of the room, diligently working.

I walked toward the balcony, figuring that was the first place I'd look for Angela since she seemed to spend most of her time there. Sure enough, there she was, gazing off into the distance.

"Angela?"

She turned, almost in slow motion. I didn't know if she was doing it for dramatic effect, or out of habit. She peered at me through her small, hooded gray eyes.

"I was thinking," I said. "If you still want my assistance, I'd be happy to do anything I can to help you find the person who, um … murdered you."

Her gray, wrinkly face remained impassive. "I had assumed I would be left alone to figure out my lot," she said. "When you reach my age—well, the age I *was*—most people don't know quite what to do with you. And that includes film directors." She made the motion of exhaling loudly without any breath coming from her. "I think I remind them that death is around the corner, and most people simply don't want to be reminded of that." A puzzled look appeared on her face. "What changed your mind?"

I shrugged. "Let's just say I realized I wanted to help, after all."

"Well, I can't say I've made much progress so far. I've spent most of my time looking out this glass door at my marquee across the street." She pointed to the neighboring hotel. "After months of a residency, who knew a performance of 'Anything Goes' at a private function would be my swan song? Followed by a swan *dive* off the balcony? Quite the interesting plot twist." She took another big, air-less breath and made the motion of rolling up her sleeves. "Well, let's get on with it, then. I'll be very helpful with the investigation, you know. I've played a detective before."

"Oh?"

She smiled broadly. "When I was very young, before I moved to the stage, I did a television series titled *Investigator*

Alley. I played the secretary to a private detective who lived on the outskirts of Alligator Alley in Florida." She patted the curls at the back of her head. "Not surprisingly, more than one body was found in the stomachs of those ghastly creatures. They do grow to be quite big, you know."

Actually, I didn't know.

"Detectives were played mainly by men back then, but in nearly every episode, I was the one who deduced who the murderer was." She said this with pride as if there were no scripts or soundstages and there had been real alligators to sidestep and real murders to solve.

"Yes, that will prove quite helpful, Angela," I said politely.

"May I help you, ma'am?"

I turned. One of the workers who had been vacuuming had stopped and switched off the machine.

"I don't think you should be so close to that door, ma'am," he said. "No one is allowed there. We have strict orders."

"Yes, I know. I was just looking for something." I reached for my phone, switched on my flashlight, and pointed to the carpeting. "I think I dropped something here this afternoon. I'm looking for it. I won't be long. I promise."

He seemed skeptical but gave a quick wave before returning to his vacuum cleaner.

"Okay," I whispered to Angela, "we don't have much time before I'm probably going to be asked to leave. Maybe you can tell me if you have any thoughts on who could have done this to you."

"Actually, I do have a suspect in mind," she said proudly.

"You do?"

"Yes, and I know where to find her. The corridor downstairs."

"Corridor?"

"Yes, the one that connects to restaurant alley. You must know it."

"No, I haven't done very much exploring while I've been here."

"For crying out loud, my dear!" Angela exclaimed. "You're a young, beautiful woman in Las Vegas! Explore!"

Um, I have a few things on my mind. "Angela, we're getting off-topic."

"Ah, yes, well, there is an upscale makeup store downstairs on the first floor, and a young woman stands outside every night, trying to shove this wrinkle eye cream in my face. She clearly despises me."

"I don't think she despises you. I think she's just trying to make a sale."

"Maybe so, but those sales associates are simply ferocious. I think they go through Navy SEAL training before working there."

"Um, any other suspects?"

Angela shook her head. "Not at all, my dear. I *am* quite beloved, you know. Ten years ago, I was voted one of America's favorite national treasures. I came in second, behind Betty White."

"Well, *I* have some thoughts."

"Do tell." Angela sounded genuinely intrigued.

"Well, I'm thinking it had to be someone at the conference. This is a closed event, right? You have to show ID and have a certain passcode to come up to the twenty-seventh floor. Unless someone was able to sneak up here undetected, that means the suspect list is only about fifty or sixty people long. Plus, another dozen more if you include the waitstaff."

"Oh, is that all?" She rolled her eyes dramatically.

"Well, at least it's a finite group. Do you know a man named Glenn Swanson?"

Angela brought her hand to her chin like Rodin's Thinker sculpture and held the pose. "I don't believe so. Should I?"

"Short, dark brown hair? Light brown eyes? I got the feeling he was lying to me when I asked him where he was when you lost your life."

"That does seem suspicious, although if everyone in the world who lied was a murderer, practically every person alive would be in prison."

I guess that's true. "Has anyone attending the conference seemed suspicious or familiar to you in any way?"

"Not in the least. But as I said, I don't really pay much attention to what happens off the stage. I am focused on my performance."

"What about the members of the dance troupe?"

"Yes, they are dears. They've been performing in my residency for the past six months. Wonderful young dancers and actresses."

"Did you remember seeing any of them right when you ... well, you know?"

She thought about it. "None that I could recall, although Teddy had walked past not more than five minutes before."

"Teddy?" The name sounded familiar. "Oh, do you mean Ted Matheson?"

"Yes, do you know him?"

"No, but he was talking to the people at my table right after the dinner show performance yesterday. I'm not sure he's a suspect, since he was standing by our table when you were supposed to have jumped from the balcony. Also, he seemed very happy to be a part of your show."

She raised her eyebrows. "Teddy is a miserable person whose best acting is done offstage."

"What do you mean?"

"I mean that he can sashay with the best of 'em when the stage lights are on, but in the day-to-day, he is quite the plodder. A miserable fellow."

"Really?" He seemed like an upbeat guy, although I knew things often weren't as they seemed. After all, Joe Turner seemed like the perfect guy to marry.

"Teddy has been trying to get my show taken away, so he can get out of his contract."

"Why?"

"I heard through the grapevine he has the opportunity to go on a national tour of some Disney show. Can you imagine?" She rolled her eyes. "Wanting to dance in a bear costume or something just as dreadful instead of appearing on stage with a Tony Award winner?" She covered her mouth with her hand as if the idea was gasp-worthy.

"You won't let him out of the contract?"

"On the contrary, I told him to go, go go, but he said it will look bad if he leaves the show. Much better to simply have it end. *Coward.*"

"Angela, are you saying that Ted might be a suspect then? Maybe he was working with someone?"

She furrowed her thin brows. "Not sure. He may be a sullen fellow, but I can't imagine him hurting a fly."

"Well, it's worth investigating. Any idea where I can find him?"

"He performs at the hotel next door after our show. He's in a lounge act."

"Got it."

The vacuum cleaning stopped, and I looked behind me. The cleaning crew was packing up their supplies. "We're running out of time. Anyone else you can think of?"

Angela narrowed her eyes. "Now that I think about it, it could be Peggy Marx."

"Who is she?"

"I'm sure you noticed her. She was the dancer whose stockings were ripped. Quite the embarrassment."

"Um, I didn't notice any ripped stockings."

Angela looked at me, astonished. "My dear, were you *watching* the performance?" She shook her head. "Well, she was the dancer with the red hair pulled into a bun."

Ah, that I *did* notice. When you were a redhead, your eyes were immediately drawn to other redheads. It was like you were in the same club, whose members were dwindling. It was only a matter of time before the recessive red-hair gene became a footnote in human history. "Why would Peggy want to murder you?"

Angela fingered the curls at the back of her head again. "Well, it is an unsavory story, and, if I say so myself, I look very unflattering in it."

"What happened?"

"You see, I was having an affair with Peggy's husband."

A tiny gasp flew from my mouth. I would have thought that after all I had seen and heard in the past six months, nothing would surprise me. Peggy looked as if she were even younger than I was. Maybe in her mid-twenties. "How old is Peggy's husband?"

Angela blinked at me with her fake-eyelashed Betty Davis eyes. "I don't know. Twenty-six, perhaps?" I must have been staring at her incredulously, because then she added, "My dear, passion knows no age."

And, apparently, no decency.

My phone pinged. I looked at it. A text from Stephanie.

"Those things are terribly disruptive," Angela said, glancing at my phone. "I never carry one."

"Sorry. It's my friend Stephanie letting me know they'll be going to some place called Bob's '50s Diner downstairs for dinner."

"Ah, yes, Bob's. I go there quite regularly," she said.

"You do?" I couldn't imagine Angela's dainty little fingers wrapped around a cheeseburger.

"Don't look so flabbergasted, my dear. Just because I enjoy Almas caviar doesn't mean I don't partake in a cheeseburger now and again."

"Miss!"

The worker who had spoken to me before was standing near the elevators with the others, the cords for their appliances neatly coiled. They looked as if they were ready to go home to their families after a long day. "Did you find what you were looking for?" he asked.

"Oh, yes. Thank you! I'll be right there!" I turned to Angela. "I'd better go. We'll talk more tomorrow, but I'll think about the things you've told me."

"Am I to remain here again tonight?" she asked with a yawn.

"I'm sorry if it's terribly lonely. But I'll be back in the morning as soon as I can."

"My dear, loneliness is a part of old age. I am unfazed by it—and unafraid of it." She turned back toward the balcony, and as she moved toward it, said, "I'll watch the bright lights of the big city until your return."

I hurried to the elevators where the worker was kindly holding the door for me.

"Thank you," I said, stepping inside.

As the doors closed and I caught a final glimpse of Angela Decatur looking out into the darkening skies of Las Vegas, it finally hit me that the bright lights that once defined her career would no longer shine upon her.

Instead, they shined *right through* her.

Chapter 13

I WALKED INTO MY hotel room and looked back at Alice's door. I wondered if she was still up. I hoped she was okay. We had both unloaded quite a bit on each other. If our conversation had taken a lot out of *me*, poor Alice must have been exhausted.

I tossed my briefcase onto the bed and was ready to hop into the shower when my phone pinged with classical music. I picked it up.

Dear Clara,

A large, flat box arrived for you. The painter was kind enough to bring it into the house. Whatever could it be? A Rembrandt painting, perhaps?

To my astonishment, this sentence was followed by a laugh emoji. *William is using emojis now? What's next? Gen Z slang?* I kept reading.

Please provide instructions. I will leave you now with a photograph of Ghost Cat standing beside the box so you can ascertain an accurate representation of its size.
Sincerely,
William

Below the text was a photo of the box leaning against the dining table. Unsurprisingly, there was no sign of Ghost Cat. But William was right. The box looked *huge*. I kicked off my shoes, sat on the bed, and leaned against the headboard. After checking my calendar, I began typing my reply.

Hi William! It's so nice to hear from you! What a day I've had... Anyway, inside that box is our new TV! Isn't that exciting? Mr. Wiggins was kind enough to give me the name of a handyman, and he is coming by tomorrow to install the TV. Mr. Wiggins will let him in. Can you do me a favor? On the underside of the kitchen drawer, all the way on the left, the one with all the forks and spoons, is an envelope. It's taped there. (Ghost Cat inspired me. She has the best hiding places!) It has money in it. Please put the envelope on the table when the handyman is done. Thank you! See you soon!

I sent the text, and no sooner did I pull out a change of clothes than my phone pinged with more music.

Dear Clara,
I shall see it done.
Sincerely,
William

I was suddenly overcome with homesickness. *How ironic*, I thought as I looked out the window at the bright lights of Las Vegas. I had been looking forward to this trip for weeks. I had been looking forward to traveling for *years*. But now that I was here, I was missing the quiet Salem streets in the morning as I walked to Derby's. I missed the good-mornings and have-a-nice-days of the folks in town. The way the sun set in Salem Common, the grassy public park. For eight years, I'd thought I was missing something by not traveling the world. And maybe I was. But right now, I was missing my dog, my friend, and my rascally ghost cat.

I turned on the TV so there would be some noise in the room while I got ready for dinner. As I clicked out of the hotel's menu, I landed on a news channel showing a journalist interviewing someone from one of those gambling sites and was suddenly reminded of Taylor Hampton—a journalist I had taken a gamble on and then found myself on the losing side of a deal.

I glanced at my watch. I had a few minutes, so I searched on my phone for the *Salem Chronicle*'s number and dialed. I didn't expect Taylor to be at the office, since it was three hours later on the East Coast, and sure enough, as soon as the phone rang on the other end, an automated voice picked up and directed me to Taylor's voicemail.

I inhaled softly as the voicemail beeped, prompting me to leave a message. *Be forceful.* "Taylor, this is Clara Kelly. It's been four weeks, and I haven't heard from you." *That's it. You got this.* "You need to hold up your end of the deal." *Or else! Tell him or else!* "And start researching a way to prove that William Kensington is innocent of everything he has been accused of." *Okay, you made your point. Now bring it home!* "I'm traveling right now, but I'll be stopping by when I get back to Salem next week." *Uh oh. Don't say it. Don't say it.* "Thank you."

I disconnected the call.

Ugh. Why did I say thank you? *Damn you, polite nature!*

But Taylor wasn't the only unfinished business I had. As I put the phone down, I thought of Angela. She had mentioned two people—Ted Matheson and Peggy Marx—as possible suspects for her murder. (I was pretty sure the wrinkle-cream lady wasn't a lead.) I'd have to check them both out tomorrow. But when? In between sessions? *Should I skip a session?*

And then there was Glenn Swanson, who I was pretty sure lied to me about where he was when Angela had been killed. But lying wasn't murder, as Angela noted. Very possibly, Glenn had been sitting on the toilet because of IBS and was just too embarrassed to say anything. Although I got the feeling that Glenn Swanson wasn't the type to be embarrassed of much. Even IBS.

My stomach rumbled. I would have to sort all this out later. Sleuthing was impossible on an empty stomach. And with that, I hurried into the shower so that I could join the others for dinner.

Chapter 14

BOB'S '50S DINER WAS hopping. (Yes, as in sock-hopping.)
I had the urge to put on my sunglasses as we walked in; the
bright tile and chrome fixtures nearly blinded me.

"Hi, do you have a reservation?!" chirped a young woman
whose nametag read *Debby* and whose smile was competing
with the fluorescent lighting for domination.

"No, we don't," Declan said. "Will that be a problem?"

Judging by the mobs waiting for a table, I had a feeling it
might be.

"Hmmm ... how big is your group, Daddy-o?" Debby
asked.

"We have six."

"Well then, you've got it made in the shade!" Debby said,
and I was beginning to wonder how many 1950s expressions
the hostess could fit into a short conversation. "Most of the

people here are groups of two and four, so you're the first six on the list, and we've got that round corner booth available." She pointed past the bar, soda fountains, and jukebox to an empty table in blue and yellow.

"We'll take it," Sissy said.

"Neat-o!" she exclaimed. "Where you cats from?"

"Salem, Massachusetts," Jonah said.

"Far out!" She pointed to a fellow hostess wearing a red-and-white soda-jerk hat. "This here is Pina. She'll take you to your table. Enjoy!"

As the rest of the group followed Pina toward the table, I decided to stop and talk to Debby, who looked familiar. I took a chance. "Are you one of the waitresses at the business conference upstairs this week?" I asked.

"Yes!" she said, appearing thrilled to be recognized. "A bunch of us who work here also work the conference. The hotel is nice enough to invite its waitstaff to apply to these kinds of positions. It's a great way to pick up some extra cash."

Great. I knew I was here for dinner, but this was a good opportunity to get some intel on Angela. I hated to turn Debby the hostess into a Debby Downer by talking about death, but I needed a lead—any lead. "By any chance, were you working the night that actress Angela Decatur ... well, when she ...?"

Debby's expression changed. She came close to me. "We're not supposed to talk about it. Management said it makes people too sad," she whispered as someone dressed as Buddy Holly jumped onto one of the counters and launched into a rendition of "Peggy Sue." The restaurant patrons clapped along.

I wasn't sure *anything* could bring the mood down in this restaurant. "But you were working that night?" I asked.

She nodded. "Yeah, but Gabriela was the one who *actually* saw her go over the ledge. Poor thing. She's still not right. The only reason she's working tonight is because she needs the money and—"

She stopped talking when a man with the word *Manager* sewn into his crisp white shirt reached into her stand and pulled out some menus. As he adjusted the toy cigarette behind his ear and wiped the dried-food residue from the menus, Debby cleared her throat and added, "Yeah, definitely, she's ... *all shook up.*" She said those last three words with a really bad Elvis impression while swiveling her hips. The manager nodded at her, satisfied, and left.

"Whew, that was a close one," Debby said. "The manager almost caught me talking about Gabriela."

"They take this 1950s vibe seriously, huh?"

"You bet. The other day, my friend Petey got fired for shaving off his Pompadour."

"Had you seen Angela Decatur in here before?" I asked, trying to circle back to the topic at hand. "I heard that she used to eat here."

"Yeah, definitely. She wasn't an every-day regular, but she came, maybe, once a month. She was always wearing sunglasses. I figured she didn't want to be recognized."

That, or she didn't want the restaurant's practically-visible-from-space lighting to damage her retinas.

A couple of tourists walked in, oohing and aahing as Buddy Holly finished his song with a flourish by tossing his plastic eyeglasses into the adoring crowd.

"Well, nice talking to you. Gotta host!" Debby said. "Enjoy your dinner!" Then she flashed the new diners her dazzling smile. "Golly gee, welcome to Bob's '50s Diner. How many in your party?"

As I made my way to the round booth in the back, I thought about what little information I was able to extract from Debby. 1) Angela was a regular customer here, which, although I knew, still struck me as strange. Buddy Holly didn't seem like her cup of tea. I saw Angela as more of a Connie Francis or Nat King Cole kinda girl. And 2) the name of the person who had seen Angela on the balcony was named Gabriela. I didn't get a chance to see Gabriela close-up that night, but I remembered her. Vividly. A pretty girl with blond hair—who was crying her eyes out.

By the time I reached our table, everyone was seated and reading the menus.

"Did you get lost?" Jonah asked me as I slid into the booth.

"No, the hostess looked familiar. Turns out, she's working the conference, too."

"I thought so!" Stephanie said. "I never forget a face."

"Did she work the night of ... you know?" Declan asked.

"Yeah," I said.

"Really?" Jonah's eyes opened wide. "Was she the one who—?"

"No, that wasn't her. Another worker saw Angela go ... well, off the ledge."

"So, we're on a first-name basis with the deceased, huh?" Jonah asked with a smile.

Um, kinda.

"I can't stop seeing the look on that poor young waitress's face," Sissy said. "Imagine seeing someone take their own life like that."

"Well, do we really know that's what happened?" I asked.

"Actually, we do," Jonah said.

"We do?"

"In today's paper, it said the police are ruling it a suicide," Sissy said.

"But," I said, stunned. "That can't be."

"Yep," Sissy said. "I know it's hard to believe."

Sissy didn't know *how* hard it was to believe. Especially when a ghost was telling you she hadn't jumped at all.

"Here." Declan showed me his phone. On the screen was the headline *Angela Decatur Death Ruled Suicide; Suicide Note Discovered in Theater Dressing Room.*

There was a suicide note?

"Great Balls of Fire" began to play, and a Jerry Lee Lewis lookalike hopped onto the bench in front of a white piano that had fake flames blowing up from its keys. People stood up and took out their cell phones.

"Wow, this place is really something, huh?" Declan said.

"Yeah, it's something all right," Stephanie said. "There's nothing on this menu that's below three thousand calories."

"What do you expect from a 1950s diner?!" Jonah shouted over the music with a laugh.

I perused the menu. I couldn't believe how hungry I was. I had barely eaten anything all day, and every mouth-watering, gazillion-calorie meal made my stomach ache with deprivation.

"What are you thinking of having, Clara?" Stephanie shouted as Jerry Lee Lewis took a bow and signed a few autographs.

"I'm thinking the double cheeseburger and fries with extra onions and a vanilla milkshake."

"That's the 1950s spirit!" Declan said. "I think I might have the same."

Our waitress came to our table and introduced herself. I was hoping it would be Gabriela, the server who had seen Angela go off the balcony, but it was an older, dark-haired woman named Wendy. As Wendy went through all the specials for the evening, I saw a nametag walk by that read *Gabriela*.

It's her.

The nametag stopped at the table next to ours and was attached to a woman I would have never recognized. At the cocktail reception, Gabriela's long, blond-highlighted hair had cascading ringlets down the sides of her face, but now her hair was in a high bun, and I could barely see it under her red-and-white soda-jerk hat.

"Miss?"

Wendy, my server, was talking to me. "Yes?"

"Would you like something to drink?" she asked.

"Oh, yes. Sorry." After I gave her my order, she nodded and left, and I resumed watching Gabriela, who was taking down the drink orders for her table on her notepad. Gabriela didn't appear distraught, as Debby the hostess had suggested. Or upset. Not that that meant anything. Most people tended to put on brave faces in public. (Some of us more than others.)

"I'll be right back with your drink orders," Gabriela said to her table.

I had to find a way to talk to her.

"So," Sissy put down her menu, "what did everyone think of their first day?"

"Frankly, I'm a little overwhelmed," Declan said.

"That's an understatement," I agreed.

"Don't worry, guys. Just take notes and don't expect to understand everything this week," Sissy said. "Also, keep in mind that a lot of these presentations will be available for download—or at least the slides, so you don't need to scribble notes constantly. Just relax and absorb as much as you can."

"It's too bad your friend Alice couldn't come tonight," Jonah said.

"Alice likes her alone time," Stephanie said.

Yeah, and now I know why. For most of her life, she had been harassed by ghosts.

"She's pretty awesome," Stephanie added.

"And she's quite an accomplished young woman," Sissy said to Jonah. "Her mother, Ellen, owns The Haunted Cookie, but Alice practically runs the place herself. And, to her credit, it's always crazy busy, so I think she's definitely earned whatever alone time she can muster."

A warm feeling came over me. How accepting these women were of Alice. And how protective. When I had run to Salem, Massachusetts, who knew I would stumble into a wonderfully generous community that not only welcomed strays but nurtured them and helped them grow into the person they needed to be? And, more than anything, I needed to *be.*

"Oh, Clara, I almost forgot." Stephanie dug into her handbag and pulled out a business card. "I ran into someone else who is setting up a bed-and-breakfast. She lives in Breckenridge, Colorado. I took her card in case you wanted to get in touch and compare notes."

"Great," I said, taking the card. "Thank you, Stephanie."

Wendy returned with our drinks and took our dinner orders. As the others began chatting about the various conference panels, I kept my eye on Gabriela. After bringing her table their drinks, she took their meal orders and then walked toward the kitchen. She ripped off the top sheet of her pad, hung it on some metal contraption with a bunch of other table orders (including ours), and headed toward the hostess stand. She whispered something to Debby and then walked out of the restaurant. *Oh no! Is her shift over?*

"I'll be right back," I said, hoping no one would ask me where I was going. Luckily, Stephanie and Declan were in the middle of a conversation, as were Sissy and Jonah, so I was able to skulk away. I wound my way around trays of three-scoop ice cream sundaes until I was out the door.

Gabriela was standing in the middle of the plaza near a grove of palm trees. I couldn't tell if the trees were fake or real, but I figured that was the fun of Las Vegas. It didn't really matter.

I tried to approach her nonchalantly, but walking across a plaza during dinnertime in Vegas was like crossing a six-lane highway. There was traffic in every direction, and I must have looked like a pinball.

Gabriela was smoking a cigarette. I was trying to figure out how I could introduce the topic of the woman she had seen fall to her death, when she looked up at me and smiled.

"Hi," she said.

"Hi."

Awkward silence.

"Do I know you?" she asked.

"Um, no," I said, fumbling for words. "I'm having dinner at Bob's."

"Oh, do you need something?"

"Well ... kinda."

"I'm on break at the moment." Gabriela held up her cigarette in case I didn't already get the hint. "I'm sure one of the other servers would be happy to get you what you need." She took a drag of her cigarette and self-consciously put it behind her back. "I don't usually smoke so much during work hours, but it's been an awful week, and my anxiety is raging." She blew out a puff of smoke.

First question that came to mind: was Gabriela's anxiety raging because she had seen Angela Decatur fall from the twenty-seventh floor of a building? Second question that came to mind: was her anxiety raging because she *pushed* Angela Decatur off the twenty-seventh floor? It was impossible to detect guilt when someone was wearing a soda-jerk hat.

"No, I don't need anything," I said, "but I was wondering if I could ask you a question."

"Sure."

"I think I recognize you from the business conference's cocktail party the other night, right?"

Gabriela's hand flew to her mouth, and she took another drag of her cigarette. "Yeah." Her hand was shaking.

"I'm so sorry. I don't mean to upset you."

"No, it's okay. My therapist said I should try and talk about it. That if I talk about it, maybe I'll be able to push through."

"I just wanted to ask you what you saw."

"I saw Angela Decatur throw herself off the ledge." She rolled her eyes. "Just like I said to the police. Why? Why do you want to know?"

Yes, genius, why do you want to know? "Well, she's someone I know." Not *knew*. Know. Not a lie.

"Oh, I'm so sorry." Gabriela's expression changed from suspicion to understanding. "How did you know her?"

"We met recently." Not a lie. "And I just don't understand why she would jump."

"People have all kinds of problems they keep from even the people they love the most. You just don't know what's going on with them."

"So, you saw her stand there and just jump off the ledge?"

"Well, not exactly."

"What do you mean?"

Gabriela took another drag of her cigarette. "She was kind of ... slumped on the ledge."

"Slumped how?"

"You know, like leaning forward. Like you do when you're depressed. Or tired. I think that's the part that bothers me the most." Another drag of her cigarette. "What if she didn't want to jump, you know? What if she was just sitting there and lost her balance or fell asleep? You know how old people can fall asleep anywhere, right? My Grandpa Jim falls asleep all the time when he's stopped at a red light. But he won't give up his license. It's crazy." Another drag. "Anyway, before I knew what was happening, she was ... well, I couldn't help her, really. I couldn't."

"Of course, you couldn't." Especially if Angela was already dead. And I was starting to think she was when Gabriela had seen her on the ledge. I didn't get the impression Gabriela was lying. Or had pushed her. But, again, *soda-jerk hat*. "Did you see anybody else on the balcony when you saw Angela?"

"No, no one. But I had just come up the stairs from the lower level."

"Stairs?"

"Yeah. There are stairs outside on the balcony that go straight to the floor below, which is where the kitchen is."

"I see."

"The only ones out there were me and Chet."

"Chet?"

"Yeah, he was the one who heard me scream and then held me. Thank God for Chet."

"Oh, I think he was my waiter. Where did Chet come from?"

"I don't know. He had a tray with food in his hand, so I assumed he came from the kitchen."

"So, no one was out there before you and Chet?" I would have to talk to this Chet guy, too.

Gabriela shook her head and took one last drag, snuffing out her cigarette on the leaf of one of the palm trees. (Note: the palm trees were fake.) "No, not that I saw. Well, I'd better get back. I'm not sure I helped you, but ..."

"No, you did," I said. "Thank you."

I followed Gabriela back into the diner (trying to look like I *wasn't* following her). Once inside, I pivoted toward the bathroom. My grand plan was to make *having to pee* my excuse for walking away from our table.

Smart thinking.

Or so I thought.

When I got inside the bathroom, Stephanie was already in there, looking at herself in the mirror. "Hey, lady, where you been?" she asked.

New grand plan. "Oh, I just went outside for a minute."

"Taking a break from this ridiculously loud '50s music?"

"Something like that." I smiled and hurried into a stall. I figured I might as well pee while I was in here.

When I came out, Stephanie asked, "What do you think of this shade of lipstick?"

I glanced at her lips, which were a spicy dark shade of red. "Pretty." I washed my hands. "I think Declan will like it."

She made a face and elbowed me playfully. "He *is* kinda cute, though, isn't he?"

"Yes." I dried my hands with a paper towel. "And he's super nice, which is even better."

Stephanie smiled, satisfied. "I've never even been to his place, Salem Blooms. I'm not really a flower person. Do you think that'll be a problem?" Her brows furrowed with concern.

"Nah," I said. "Has he taken one of your tours?"

"No."

"Well, then you're even."

"I like the way you think, Clara Kelly."

As we walked out of the bathroom, and I prepared myself to scarf down my cheeseburger, I heard someone say, "Clara Kelly, right?"

Stanley Paulson was standing near one of those old cigarette machines with the knobs.

"Stanley, hi," I said, flustered.

"Sorry, I don't usually stand right outside a restaurant's restroom," his cheeks reddened, "but I'm waiting for Kurt Walker."

"Oh, no worries," I said. "It's fine."

"Clara, you haven't introduced me to your *friend*?" Stephanie held out her hand, her newly dark-red lips curving into a smile.

"Oh. Stephanie Hastings," I said. "This is Stanley Paulson."

They shook hands.

"You can call me Stanley," he said, adding, "You both can." He smiled at me. "Kurt was telling me I had to try Bob's Diner, and I have to say, it didn't disappoint."

"Yeah, this place is definitely a must-see," Stephanie said with a laugh.

"Well," I said, "we'd better head back to our table. I'm sure the food—"

"There's *plenty* of time, Clara," Stephanie interrupted. "I'm sure the food hasn't even arrived yet. I'll tell you what. I'll go check. You stay here and visit with your *friend*. I'll text you if it's there. Nice to meet you, Stanley." She waltzed away, adding, "Take your time, Clara!"

Um, if Stephanie was trying not to be obvious, she was doing a poor job of it.

"Well, she seems fun," Stanley said, watching Stephanie go.

"She's great."

We smiled at each other, and I would have said there was an awkward silence between us, but the music was way too loud to call it that. *Awkward noise?*

"Kurt tells me Elvis Presley will be out in a few minutes doing one of his popular numbers," Stanley said. "Kurt was supposed to be having dinner with his wife tonight, but she's feeling under the weather, and he asked me to join him. I don't know if that was lucky for me or lucky for her."

I laughed as Kurt Walker exited the bathroom.

"Kurt, this is Clara Kelly," Stanley said. "A soon-to-be bed-and-breakfast power broker. She's attending the conference."

"Ah, yes. The name rings a bell," Kurt said. "Are you enjoying it so far, Ms. Kelly?"

"Yes, very much. Thank you. I learned a lot today."

"Well, that's what we're here for."

A voice came over an unseen loudspeaker. "Ladies and gentlemen, and now the man you've been waiting for ..."

A commotion was taking place near the stage as diners left their tables with their phones in hand.

"Well, looks like Elvis is in the building," Kurt Walker shouted over the noise. "This guy is a pretty good impersonator. We've used him several times for our conferences." He turned to me. "It was nice meeting you, Clara. Enjoy the rest of the conference."

"Thank you," I said.

"Yes, nice to run into you again, Clara," Stanley said.

"You too, Stanley," I said as he nodded and walked off.

As music began to play and Elvis took the stage, Stanley called, "I hope you're able to check out my panel tomorrow, Clara. As I said, I'd be happy to answer any questions you have."

Then the two men disappeared into the crowd just as Elvis launched into a rendition of "Burning Love" and Wendy, my waitress, appeared near the kitchen with a tray of food in her hands.

Was I finally going to eat?!

As the crowd surged toward the stage to see a pair of swiveling hips in a bejeweled white jumpsuit, I fought my way in the other direction—like a salmon swimming up-stream—toward a delicious vanilla shake and *a hunk, a hunk* of burger with my name on it.

Chapter 15

"A SUICIDE NOTE?!" ANGELA said, appalled, when I arrived in the ballroom early the next morning, about a half hour before the conference breakfast was set to begin. "Well, that's absurd."

I showed Angela the news story on my phone.

"Like I can *see* that teeny-tiny type with my eyes," she scoffed. "Death has done nothing to improve my vision. Plus, I don't care what that *device* says." She tried to push the phone away, but her wrinkled gray hand kept moving through it. "That note is clearly fraudulent."

I pointed to the screen. "It says they checked the handwriting. They compared it to some other things, like autographs, you'd written. It's yours."

"I'm telling you that's not possible," Angela said. "Where did they find the note? What did it say?"

I scrolled the news story. "I don't know what it said, but it was found in your dressing room, it says. On your vanity."

"How poetic." Angela switched to theater mode, the back of her hand against her forehead. "The vain actress who was losing her looks due to age penned her final missive on a vanity table—before throwing herself off a ledge following her final performance," she said dramatically. "Oh, what I would have given to play that role."

"Okay." I put my phone away. "If the note wasn't put there by you, then who did it? Is there anyone who had access to your dressing room?"

"My dear," she said, rolling her eyes, apparently frustrated with my lack of theater knowledge. "It's a dressing room, not Fort Knox. Yes, there are locks and keycards and all that nonsense, but nothing in life is foolproof, which is why I don't keep any personal effects there. A lot of snooping eyes."

"So, maybe someone slipped the note onto your vanity the night of your death. To make your death look like a suicide."

"Quite possible."

"Maybe we should check it out?"

"I beg your pardon."

"You know, the two of us go over to the theater and have a look around. You can tell me if anything looks suspicious."

"You mean, right now?"

"Well, not *now*." I looked at my watch. "I can't stay long."

Angela narrowed her eyes at me, but before she could say *rocking chair* about my coming and going so much, I added, "I told my friend I'd meet her at her hotel room this morning."

"You mean I'm able to leave this place?" she asked.

I nodded my head. "Yes, I'll help you. You haven't learned yet to manipulate physical objects—"

"My dear, I have no desire to learn *anything* at this stage of my life. Or my afterlife."

How interesting. William seemed eager to learn new things and was fascinated by technology. Angela, not so much. "Well, like I said, I'll help you." I walked toward the large balcony windows, where the morning sun was shining brightly. "I was talking to one of the waitresses last night at dinner. Her name is Gabriela." I pointed to a spot on the balcony outside. "That's where she was standing when she saw you leaning over the ledge."

"I don't remember leaning over the ledge."

"My theory is that you were dead before you got there. The murderer must have placed you there." I pointed to another section of the balcony. "See that area there? It's out of view from just about anyone inside." I faced her. "What's the last thing you remember?"

"I remember someone grabbing me from behind and placing their hands over my nose and mouth." For the first time, Angela looked uncomfortable, recalling the events that led to her death. "I remember struggling and then nothing. I was standing outside when that young waitress began to scream."

"Could it have been that young waitress who grabbed you?"

"I don't know. Do you suspect her?"

"Not really." I shrugged.

Angela assumed the Thinker position again. "I believe you're right, though. I was dragged backward toward this area." She pointed to the section I had indicated, a tiny alcove. Could that have been where the murderer was hiding? Or had he come up the set of stairs Gabriela mentioned? Or had the murderer walked right onto the balcony from the ballroom? I tried to open the door to the balcony, but it was locked.

"What are you doing?" Angela asked.

"I was hoping I could get outside, take a look around." I pointed to the alcove. "The murderer could have killed you there and then positioned you on the ledge in such a way that gravity pulled you over the side."

"Ah, gravity. It is certainly not kind to women," Angela lamented.

"I'm not sure whoever murdered you was counting on Gabriela seeing you go over, but that ended up being fortuitous for them because Gabriela corroborated that your death was a suicide." Unless she was covering for the murderer. But my gut told me that wasn't the case.

I smooshed my cheek against the cool glass and peered out the window. I didn't see anything helpful. Like a footprint. Or a note from the killer with a photo ID. (That would have been *really* helpful.) But I did notice something reflective on the ground.

"What's that?" I asked.

"What's what?"

"There's something there. It's small and round, but I can't see it too well." I quickly reached for my phone, zoomed in the screen, and then held it near the glass, snapping several photos.

I looked at the images. The first three were blurry. Ugh. But the fourth was clear and showed a small black object with tiny holes wedged into the corner of the balcony.

"What *is* that?" I asked Angela, zooming in on the photo for her old, ghostly eyes.

"It looks like a button."

I looked again at the screen. It *was* a button. Was this a clue?

"Is a button earth-shattering?" Angela asked.

"I don't know. But it could have been worn by the murderer. Maybe it came off during the struggle between the two of you. Was there a struggle?"

"My dear, at my age, *everything* is a struggle." Angela shook her head. "And I don't mean to burst your sleuthing bubble, but that button could have been there for years. For all we know, it was worn by Frank Sinatra or another member of the Rat Pack in the 1960s."

Maybe. But maybe not. I wondered if the police had overlooked it. Or if it had blown there or was tossed from an upper floor *after* the murder took place. I tried taking a few more photos to see if there were any identifying marks on the button, but there were none. A small, plain black button.

"You know, my dear, you may be on to something, after all," Angela said.

"You think?"

"I was in a play just a few years ago titled *Sea No Evil*—yes, I know, a dreadful name—and the murderer was detected based on DNA analysis of his saliva, which was found on a lobster bib he had been wearing at dinner at a seafood restaurant that night."

I wasn't seeing the connection. "Are you saying you think the murderer's *saliva* might be on that button?"

Angela appeared indignant. "Well, it's a long shot, yes, but stranger things have happened."

She had a point. I looked at my watch. "I'd better go. I'll catch up with you later today, around lunchtime, and we'll take a walk over to the theater. Meet me near the elevators around noon."

"Oh, how exciting!" Angela said, clasping her gray hands together. "A real-life murder mystery."

I was glad *someone* was excited.

As I walked toward the elevators, Kurt Walker appeared, carrying a tray with coffee and a Danish pastry. When he saw me, he seemed surprised. "Ah, Clara, is it? You're up bright and early this morning."

"Yes." *Think, think...* "For some reason, I thought I was meeting my friend up here to go over notes, but I realize now we're supposed to meet in her room." For a woman who wanted to begin living her truth, lying was becoming an everyday thing for me.

An elevator opened in front of us, and Kurt held the door. "After you," he said. "I'm on my way down to meet my wife. She's a late sleeper."

"I hope she's feeling better. Stanley mentioned she was under the weather."

"Yes, this is for her." He motioned to his tray, and in the center was a small vase with a flower. "I'm hoping it will perk her up a little."

How sweet. I stepped into the elevator.

"What floor?" Kurt asked, walking in behind me.

"Fifth."

As he pushed the button with the number 5, lighting it up, my breath hitched.

"Is everything okay?" he asked.

"Um, yeah. Fine," I said.

A lie.

"Are you sure?"

"Yes."

Another lie.

Because as Kurt Walker's hand left the fifth-floor button to press the sixth-floor button, which must have been his floor, I noticed the arm of his jacket sleeve.

It was detailed with two black buttons. And a knot of thread in between.

Which meant one of the buttons was missing.

And was very possibly lying in the corner of the twenty-seventh-floor balcony.

Chapter 16

Kurt Walker? A murderer? He seemed to genuinely care for Angela Decatur. I knew appearances could be deceiving, but could I be that duped?

And then there was my immediate problem: *I am quite possibly stuck in an elevator with a vicious killer.*

Luckily, Kurt seemed absorbed in arranging and then rearranging the flower in the vase on his tray and not the least bit interested in snuffing the life out of me. When the elevator doors opened on the sixth floor, he smiled, uttered a chipper *Have a nice day*, and hardly even noticed I was clutching my purse, ready to use it as a quasi-blunt object, if need be.

The elevator doors closed. *Have I just escaped death?*

On the fifth floor, I bolted out of the elevator and hurried down the hallway toward Stephanie's hotel room as if at any moment Kurt Walker would change his mind about letting me go and chase after me with a meat cleaver.

I knocked a little too hard on Stephanie's door, and when she opened it, she looked at me strangely. "Clara, are you all right? Are you sweating?"

"Um, I'm fine! Just thought I'd get a little cardio in before the conference," I said, jogging in place and pumping my arms.

"*O-kay.* I thought maybe it was indigestion from that burger last night." Stephanie wrinkled her nose. "I think that was more meat than I've had in about two years." She closed the hotel door behind her. "Are you ready for another day of adventure?"

Um, she had no idea.

We waited by the elevators for quite a while. Probably lots of traffic going up to the twenty-seventh floor, and each time an elevator opened, it was too full for us to fit. I was hoping an empty one would arrive soon because I was still jogging in place to keep up the act and was getting tired. Finally, one arrived that was only half full, and we stepped inside.

We went up only one floor when the elevator stopped. As the doors opened, Kurt Walker was standing in front of me. The tray in his hands was gone and in its place was a pile of papers. *Is he planning on collating me to death? Death by paper cut?*

"Clara Kelly, we meet again," he said, smiling.

I tried not to think that was *exactly* the kind of thing the villain would say to the hero in every movie I'd ever seen.

A woman was standing next to Kurt. "This is my wife, Deidre," Kurt said, stepping into the elevator. A few of the people in the elevator oohed and aahed, excited to be so close to our business conference leader. If they knew what *I* knew, they would be cowering in fear.

Deidre gave me a not-too-friendly smile and nod before walking into the elevator and turning around so that her back was facing me. She looked to be in her forties. Her highlighted blond hair was perfectly styled and blown out, like she had just come from an appointment at the salon—not lying in bed, sick as a dog. Her perfume permeated the small space, making my nostrils itch.

"Are we all enjoying the conference?" Kurt asked as he pushed the *Door Close* button with his button-less jacket sleeve.

"Dear," Deidre said with a huff, "I told you at the cocktail party that you shouldn't wear this jacket again until I could bring it to the tailor." She exhaled dramatically and disapprovingly.

Kurt had worn this jacket to the cocktail party? The night Angela was killed? I took a teeny-tiny step away from Kurt.

"You know it's my favorite jacket, dear," Kurt said.

He wore his favorite jacket to a murder? I took another teeny-tiny step.

"But there's a button missing." Deidre shook her head like such a thing was inexcusable. For a woman who didn't have a hair out of place, it probably was.

Suddenly, Kurt reached into his jacket pocket, and I was sure he was going to pull out some weapon and do away with all of us, but when he opened his hand, a small black button was in his palm.

"See, I have the button," he said to Deidre. "I've been meaning to get it fixed. I'll go down to the tailor today at lunchtime. Promise." He kissed her cheek.

Wait, so the button on the balcony on the twenty-seventh floor wasn't Kurt's? Or did he go up there and snatch it while I was jogging in place on the fifth floor?

When the elevator door opened, and Kurt and Deidre walked out of the elevator, I sprinted toward the balcony.

"You're still running, Clara?" Stephanie asked.

"Getting in my steps!" I called.

When I reached the balcony windows, Angela blinked her hooded eyes at me. "Back so soon?" she asked.

But there was no time to explain. I looked down at the alcove, expecting the little black button—the one possible clue I had found so far—to be gone, but there it was. Still in the corner.

It isn't Kurt Walker's.

Relief washed through me. Mixing with the thin sheen of sweat that was beginning to form on my skin from all the running. Yet, two questions remained: 1) if that black button wasn't Kurt Walker's, whose was it? And 2) did it have anything to do with Angela's murder?

WHEN THE MORNING SESSION ended and the conference broke for lunch, I looked for Angela near the elevators, as planned. She was there, trying to sidestep the conference attendees walking through her, making her look like she was doing a country-style dance in slow motion. When all the people cleared out, she saw me, looking relieved.

"I trust you had a good, informative morning, my dear. Did you learn much about bed-and-breakfasting?"

I put my earbuds in my ears. "I did. It was a panel about networking."

"Such an odd word. *Networking*. Makes it sound like you're plugged into a power grid."

"In some ways, that's what networking is, I guess. Getting your power from the support of others." I smiled. "Are you ready for our field trip?"

"As ready as I'll ever be," Angela said. "Are you sure I can just walk right into the elevator?"

"Yes, you should be fine."

"Forgive me if I'm not so confident in your use of the word *should*."

Truth be told, neither was I, but my experience with ghosts told me this *should* work. And my last panel was all about exuding confidence in social situations, so here I was practicing already.

As the elevator doors opened and I was about to go inside, Stephanie zoomed past me and got into the elevator first. "Hey, lady," she said. "Aren't you having lunch?"

"Um, I thought I might go for a walk outside."

"In this heat?" Stephanie said. "You're a brave woman."

"What about you? You're not eating?"

"I am," she said. "My phone is dying, and I left my charger in my room."

"Oh." I stepped into the elevator as Stephanie pushed the button for the fifth floor. "Lobby?" she asked.

I nodded, and as the doors began to close, I reached out my hand to stop them.

"What are you doing?" Stephanie asked.

"Oh, I thought I heard someone shout for us to hold the elevator."

We waited, even though I knew no one was coming, and I hoped Angela would get the hint, but she just stood there.

"You can get in," I said finally, and she slowly moved into the elevator car, her long dress following behind her.

"Who are you talking to?" Stephanie asked.

"Oh, there was a woman back there who looked like she needed the elevator, but she changed her mind."

Finally, when Angela was next to me, I let go of the elevator doors, which closed, and the elevator began to go down.

"Oh, how about that, my dear. You're right. I'm descending," Angela said with joy. "Let's just hope I stop at the lobby and don't continue into the pits of hell." She chuckled at her own joke.

"Hey, I saw your friend *Stanley*," Stephanie said, batting her eyelashes.

"Very funny," I said.

"He asked for you. Said he had a panel this afternoon and wanted to remind you." That was the second reminder, after the one he gave me last night. Either Stanley Paulson *really* wanted me to come to his session or he thought I had short-term memory loss. "Are you going to go?"

"I'm not sure," I said. "There are some other things I want to do."

"Like call *William*?" Stephanie nudged me.

"Who's William?" Angela asked.

"Funny," I said to Stephanie.

"Was I being funny?" Angela asked.

My body may have been going down, but my head was spinning.

"Oh, and it looks like Alice is feeling better," Stephanie said. "I saw her coming out of a session about podcasting."

I smiled. That was good news. Alice had come out of hiding and was living her life—despite the fact there was at least one ghost roaming the twenty-seventh floor.

"Your friend has a lovely complexion," Angela said when we arrived at the fifth floor. "However, her taste in fashion is questionable. That jacket looks like a child's finger-painting exercise."

Speaking of children, when the doors opened, a pair of toddlers came running into the elevator and right through Angela.

"My word!" Angela said, lifting her ghostly arms.

My stomach clenched at the thought that the children might be able to see Angela, but they didn't seem to. They were too preoccupied with the elevator buttons, pushing all of them with chocolaty fingers.

"Boys, boys, you should have let these nice people out of the elevator first," said a harried mother standing outside the elevator as Stephanie stepped out.

"I'll see you later, Clara," Stephanie said. "Enjoy your walk."

"Thanks!" I said. "See you later!"

The mother got in the elevator, and the doors closed.

"They really are very sweet boys," the mother told me, apologetically. She took out a disinfectant wipe and cleaned the elevator buttons.

"That's what they *all* say," Angela said with a roll of her eyes. "Parents are quite oblivious to how annoying their children are."

When we got to the lobby, the toddlers went running off into the casino, chased by their mother, who uttered an anxious goodbye. I held the door for Angela as several people filed in.

"Thank you," one woman said to me, walking right through Angela.

"My word, please watch where you're going," Angela said to her.

"She can't hear you," I whispered.

"Excuse me?" the woman in the elevator asked.

"Oh, I said, 'Enjoy the rest of your day.'"

The woman smiled. "Thank you," she said as the elevator doors closed. "You as well."

"Let's walk this way," I said to Angela, adjusting my earbuds.

Angela was still watching the children who had been in our elevator. They were pushing buttons on a vacant Joker Poker slot machine. "I can't remember when they started letting children into casinos," she said. "Horrible decision."

"I take it you don't have any children."

"Children?!" Angela looked appalled. "Good God, no."

I couldn't help but laugh. "You make it seem like a death sentence."

"In the 1960s, for a young stage actress, it certainly was. Do *you* have children?"

"No, I have a dog, though. And a ghost cat."

"Well, if I had the option of having *ghost* children, maybe I would have taken the plunge. Otherwise, I'm just not the mothering kind. No, no, no ..." She waved her hand. "It was hard enough making it in this business without children. Had I been strapped to a litter of suckling petri dishes, I would have never been able to work."

Angela followed me to the front of the lobby and into the large revolving door, which, luckily, was revolving slowly enough to match her walking speed. Once outside, the dry, hot air slapped against my cheeks.

"I can't believe the temperature here," I said. "It's like an oven."

"You get used to it, my dear. You can get used to *anything*."

Well, not *anything*. I thought of Joe.

The hotel next door, where Angela performed her residency, wasn't a far walk, but with Angela's small, precise steps, it took us about a half hour. I pretended to look up at the buildings and pulled out my camera so people would think I was slow-walking because I was sightseeing. I breathed a sigh of relief when we entered the hotel because I was sweating like a pig.

"Do you need a moment to powder your nose?" Angela asked when she took a good look at me.

"No, I'm fine."

Angela raised her eyebrows to convey that, no, I certainly wasn't fine, but if I wanted to walk around looking like swine, that was my business.

"Where is the theater located?" I asked.

"Right this way," Angela said. "It's off the right corridor from the lobby."

I let Angela lead since she seemed to enjoy the opportunity—and because I didn't mind lingering in the subzero air conditioning—and we followed the signs for the Angela K. Decatur Theater.

"I didn't know the theater was named after you," I said. "How exciting."

"Isn't it grand?" she said, a sparkle in her gray eyes. "The dedication was in the spring of last year. There was a mention of it on *Entertainment Tonight*."

The corridor featuring the theater, a French restaurant, and a make-your-own-candy store that was closed for renovations was tucked away in a quiet spot, far from the chaos of the hotel casino. Angela pointed at the candy store.

"In the early 1980s, when Geraldine Ferraro was all the rage in politics, I starred in a very underrated play titled *Politics Makes Strange Marshmallows*. I would ask you if you've heard of it, but hardly anyone has. I played a candymaker who finds herself running for president," she said. "I got a standing ovation on opening night. Unfortunately, the play closed the next day. Perhaps it was just too sophisticated for the audiences of that day and age. Pity." She walked past a large, lighted sign featuring her portrait, which was dimmed; flowers were scattered around it on the floor.

"This is all I guess I'm worth. A few scattered petals." Angela *humphed* and directed me to the closed theater doors.

"Wait, you want me to ... just open the doors to the theater?" I asked.

"Well, my dear, unless the two of us can figure out how to walk through walls, I'm afraid it's the only way."

"But won't I get into trouble?"

"Probably," she said. "But anything worth doing is worth getting into trouble."

I took a breath and searched the corridor. There was nobody around. Then I pulled open the door, expecting it to be locked, but it swung toward me easily. "They don't lock these? Isn't there concern that people are going to go in?"

"Dear, nobody cares about a theater in a casino in the daylight hours."

I quickly held the door open, giving Angela time to waltz inside with her long train, and then let it shut behind us.

Inside, the theater was dark. And quiet. But even without much light, I could see how beautiful it was. Like an old Broadway theater with elaborate plasterwork and elegant ornamentation.

"How do we get backstage?" I asked Angela, who was gliding down the center aisle. "Angela?"

She walked past the front row and toward the side of the stage, ascending a series of steps. Then she walked to center stage and turned to face the empty seats.

"How ironic that this is where I've always felt the most alive," Angela said, taking a bow. "And yet here I am, quite dead."

As I walked down the carpeted aisle, watching Angela, I thought again of my mother and our trips to New York City to see Broadway shows. How special those afternoons were. "Did you come from a theater-loving family?" I asked.

Angela shook her head. "No, not at all. My family ... well, we didn't have the money for those types of things. I was the youngest of nine children—six of whom died at an ungodly young age. Before they turned three." Angela began to pace on the stage as if giving a soliloquy. "My oldest sister died of tuberculosis at age seven. And my other sister died in an automobile accident when she was sixteen."

"Oh my gosh." I sat down in one of the first-row seats. "I'm so sorry."

"Alas, it's the way it goes sometimes," she said. "Although having people close to me die suddenly has rather affected me. And my relationships. If I can call them that. The parade of psychologists I've seen over the years refer to it as the anxiety associated with separation anxiety, what they liked to call AASA."

"I've never heard of AASA."

"I would assume you wouldn't have as I believe I am the only one to have had it."

"So, you don't have any family at all? Aunts? Uncles? Cousins?"

"My dear, I'm nearly eighty years old," she said. "I am the last withering branch on the Decatur family tree." She raised her thin eyebrows. "My mother was the last to go. She died in 1984." Her eyes wandered from me to the empty seating. "She had just seen me in *Pop Goes the Damsel*, a film I co-starred with action-star Buck Swagger. Do you know it?"

I shook my head.

"It's about a young secretary who becomes stuck in a giant popcorn machine and the dashing young usher who saves her." She took one of those no-air inhales I had become accustomed to ghosts taking. "What can I say? It was the 1980s, and money made us do stupid things."

My phone pinged.

"My dear, you're supposed to silence your phones in a theater." Angela rolled her eyes.

"Sorry." I pulled out my phone and was surprised to see a text from Taylor Hampton. Was he *finally* responding? Could we finally get the ball rolling on exonerating William?

Angela seemed to be occupying herself for the moment, so I quickly read Taylor's text:

Media inquiries and appearance requests should be sent to my publicist.

This was followed by the name and email address of a public relations agency in Salem, Massachusetts.

Was he kidding? He was directing me to a publicist? He wasn't going to answer me directly? I didn't think it was possible for Taylor Hampton's ego to be any bigger than it was when I first met him, but it had ballooned since I last saw him at Wyatt House. I wanted to tell him where he could put his publicist, but I needed him to help me clear William's name. I would deal with him later.

"C'mon, Angela, let's find your dressing room."

She led me stage right and down a narrow corridor to a series of rooms. It was dark—horror-movie dark—and my belly was filled with butterflies. "What if they find me in your dressing room?" I whispered. "Can't they arrest me?"

"Well, then don't let them find you, my dear," she said plainly.

Good talk.

She led me to a door that had a star in glittery gold with her name etched onto it.

"My home away from home," she said. "My makeup. My gowns." She sighed. "To think, I will never occupy it—"

Bang!

"What was that?" I whispered.

Angela put her hands on her elegant gray hips. "Clearly, someone is inside *my* dressing room," she said indignantly.

"Maybe it's the killer," I whispered.

"For what reason? To put *another* suicide note on my vanity?" she asked and narrowed her eyes at me. "Well, don't just stand there. Open the door and see."

Just walk in on a killer? Easy for *her* to say. She was already dead.

I reached for the doorknob, and there were more noises. Drawers opening. Slight grunting. Someone was definitely inside. I pulled my hand away.

"Oh, for Pete's sake." Angela reached out, grabbed the doorknob, turned it, and pulled. And before I could congratulate her on figuring out how to manipulate a physical object, my eyes landed on Ted Matheson, the guy from Angela's dance troupe, who was sitting at Angela's vanity, wearing a long purple gown and applying mascara to his eyelashes.

Chapter 17

"Just what do you think you're doing?" Angela and Ted demanded simultaneously. I was standing in the doorway, waiting for Ted to respond, when I suddenly remembered he hadn't heard Angela's question—and that he was waiting for *me* to answer *his*.

What am I doing here? My mind went blank.

"You better leave before I call the police," Ted said smugly.

I turned to go, but Angela bellowed, "Don't you leave!"

I stopped.

"Excuse me," Ted said. "I said I was going to call the police."

"No, he won't," Angela said. "This isn't the first time I caught him trying on my dresses. I've told him before. He'll stretch them out. Plus, he doesn't have any right to be in here."

"That's it." Ted picked up a cell phone and began pressing buttons.

"Tell him that if he calls the police," Angela said, "you'll tell them to check the locker in his dressing room."

I tried to get my mouth to say the words. But they wouldn't come out.

"C'mon, dear, use your strong indoor voice," Angela coaxed.

"Um ..." My cheeks warmed. "If you call the police, I'll tell them to check the locker in your dressing room."

Ted's face changed from angry to aghast. He put the phone down. "How do you know about that?"

"Um ..." *How do I know about that?* I glanced at Angela, hoping she would feed me a line, but she didn't. "That's ... That's not important," I stammered. "What's important is that I know."

"That's my girl," Angela said. "Improvisation is one of the hardest things to master. You are quite the quick study." She moved about the room, looking around. "My Lord, he's made himself at home here. While my corpse is still unburied." She rolled her eyes. "Such a savage business this is."

"Why are you here?" Ted asked.

Great. Another good question.

I glanced at Angela for a little help, but she was still in acting-school mode, wanting me to figure out the script myself.

Before I could answer, Ted said, "Wait, you look familiar to me."

"Yes, we've met. I was at the business conference. The one where Angela ..."

"That's right," he said. "I remember you now. You're hard to forget with that red hair. It's quite a lovely shade. What brand do you use?"

"Brand?"

"Hair dye, of course," Ted tutted.

"I don't use hair dye. This is my natural shade."

"Of course it is," he said sarcastically. "Whatever. What are you doing here?"

"I could ask you the same thing. And you're rummaging through all of Angela's things. And wearing her dress."

"How do you know this isn't mine?" he asked, posing.

"Well ..." This Ted Matheson was pretty good at improvisation. I looked around the room and pointed. "See? Angela's wearing it in that photo over there."

"Very good, young Clara," Angela said. "Use the space. Use what you see."

"Fine," Ted said. "It's not mine. But why shouldn't I get it now that she's gone? She has no family and no one else to inherit her things. You think someone from the Salvation Army will wear this? Please. Plus, that woman was *wretched*. It's no surprise she offed herself."

"I *was* not and *did* not," Angela said, indignant.

"Do you know she had an affair with Peggy's husband?" he asked. "One of the young women in our dance troupe?"

I glanced at Angela, but she looked away.

"It turned out to be for the best, luckily." Ted pulled at the top of his cheeks until they were red; he glanced at his reflection. "Peggy is in a *wonderful* relationship now. But if Angela had decided to jump off a ledge a few years back, it would have saved Peggy some aggravation."

So, this Peggy person was happy now? In a new relationship? Happy people tended not to commit murder. Or so I thought. Maybe it wasn't her. But that didn't rule out Ted. "You don't seem too broken up about Angela's passing," I said. "And yet you seemed so enamored with her at the business conference."

"That's called *acting*," he said with a sniff.

"So, you're happy she's gone?"

"Yes, *thrilled*," he said sarcastically. "Considering now I'm out of a job."

"Wait, I thought you wanted the show to close so you could go off and do your Disney thing?"

"Yeah, well, that fell through a few days ago." He looked at me. "How did you know about *that*?"

Panic. Instant. "Theater gossip. You know how it is. Plus, everyone knows you were destined for bigger and better things."

"Attagirl," Angela said with a nod. "Telling men exactly what they want to hear was how I managed the first third of my career."

And also how I managed eight years of marriage to Joe.

"Well, *obviously*, I'm destined for bigger things," Ted said, putting the mascara back into a small toiletry bag. "You know, Angela and I didn't see eye to eye on many things ..."

"Most things," Angela said.

"But I really learned a lot from her. How to handle myself. How to fight for myself in this cutthroat business. I have an audition for a musical in New York City to become a member of Sutton Foster's dance troupe. I'm experimenting with some makeup and wardrobe choices." He motioned to the gowns behind him. "Thought I'd come in here and maybe Angela's success would rub off on me. It's time for a change." He blinked his heavily mascaraed eyes. "So, what are you doing here, exactly?"

I couldn't tell him I was there to snoop for clues to Angela's murder. "I was a big fan and thought I'd, you know, come and pay my respects."

"By breaking and entering?"

"The door was open."

He nodded. "I was surprised, actually, at how little reaction there was to her death. Angela's residency was, by most accounts, a wild success, and yet when she died, there didn't seem to be an adequate response. People just move on, I guess." He looked at his reflection in the mirror, turning his head from side to side. "When one show closes, another opens. Like I said, a brutal business."

I stood there, fidgeting. What was I supposed to do now? I couldn't start opening drawers and rummaging through closets. Not with Ted Matheson here. "Well, I didn't mean to disturb you, even though you're not supposed to be in here, either," I said. "Good luck with your audition in New York."

"That's it?" Angela asked. "You're not going to browbeat him with questions?" She sighed heavily. "Clearly, you need to work on your interrogation tactics."

"Good luck to you as well," Ted said, zipping his toiletry bag closed. "You know, this is where it was found." He indicated a spot in front of him on the mirror.

"Where what was found?" I asked.

"The suicide note."

"There *was* no suicide note," Angela insisted.

Ted was pointing just under an early headshot of Angela that was tucked into the vanity. She must have been only twenty-five years old in the photo. How interesting to see how a face changed over the years. I could still see remnants of that youth in Angela's gray, wrinkled expression.

"I was the one who found it," Ted said.

"You did? What did it say?"

"Aren't *you* the curious one."

"Oh, stop with the suspense-building, for crying out loud," Angela said.

I crossed my arms.

"Oh, all right." Ted sighed. "I guess there's no harm in telling you." He paused again, apparently still trying to build suspense. "It said, 'I'm so very sorry. But it is for the best. I hope you understand one day.' Poignant, no?" He stood up. "Anyway, can you do me a favor before you go? Can you unzip me?" He turned around. "I managed to get this dress on, but I can't seem to get the darn thing off."

"Sure, I guess." As I undid the long zipper on Ted's dress, I thought about the words on the suicide note and what they meant. I glanced at Angela, wondering if she had any ideas, but she appeared stunned, looking off into space, her wrinkled face a pale gray.

As if she had suddenly seen a ghost.

Chapter 18

As we left the dressing room, Angela was still in some kind of trance. "It can't be," she said. "It just can't be."

"What?" I asked. "What are you thinking?"

"But it was so long ago."

"What was so long ago?"

We were back in the dark theater, walking up the center aisle. I hurried in front of her as we neared the back row. "Please tell me," I said.

Angela stood there, uncertain. "Frankly, I haven't told this to a soul. And I'm not sure I want to tell it now."

"Angela, if it has something to do with your murder ..."

"But, how could it?" She took a deep, breathless inhale and then nodded. "You may want to sit," she said.

I sat down in an aisle seat of the back row.

"Well," she hesitated, "perhaps I should start by saying that what I told you before wasn't *entirely* accurate."

"Which part?"

"The part about having no children."

A jolt of electricity went through me. "What do you mean?"

She brought her hand to her chest theatrically. "I did ... have a child." She paused, and I wondered if it was out of habit as a theater actress, giving her audience a chance to gasp or absorb the information. "This was in the 1970s. Birth control for women was on the rise, and I was taking the pill. And happily so. But for some reason, it didn't *take* to me."

"You got pregnant?"

"Yes. Not surprising, I suppose, as children—and many of them—seem to run in my family. But I never intended to be a mother. And didn't plan on becoming one then. I told myself, at the time, that I couldn't let children interfere with my burgeoning career. But if I were to be truthful ... I was also fearful to have a child. Fearful that my child would die young like my siblings had. And I just couldn't bear that kind of pain again."

"So, what did you do?"

"I thought, of course, about having an abortion. It was no secret that many of my fellow actresses were having them. The pregnancy was coming at an especially inopportune time. I had just won my first Tony for *Plane Jane*, playing the wife of a philandering congressman who decides to throw caution to the wind, so to speak, and become a pilot so that she can fly food and supplies to impoverished communities in Louisiana." She looked at me with a smile. "Frank Rich at the *Times* said my Cajun accent was very authentic, you know."

"Angela, we're losing focus."

"In theater parlance, such information is called an *aside*."

"Yeah, well, in a murder investigation, it could be called obstruction of justice."

"Yes, yes, all right. Well, I had made it all the way to the clinic. I was wearing a disguise and everything so as not to be recognized." She put her hand to her chin. "I do wonder what happened to that blond wig ..."

Blond wig? My thoughts went to Boy, who was at The Pampered Pup, probably missing his blond wig. I should have brought it with his other toys.

Great, now *I* was losing focus.

"To make a dreadfully long story short, I decided against the abortion," Angela said. "Although the pregnancy was coming at an inopportune time, it was also a good time as I was inundated with roles after that Tony win. Everyone suddenly wanted Angela Decatur to bring some sophistication and prestige to their project." Her gray eyes crinkled as she smiled. "And the parts were simply magnificent. Brian De Palma sought me out specifically for a project he was being asked to do—a theatrical release about Lady Macbeth." She clapped her hands together. "Joy! Men were finally realizing that it was *Lady Macbeth* who was the most interesting character in that bloody Shakespeare play." She sighed and dropped her hands. "But with the pregnancy, I had to pass. Incidentally, that project fell apart without me, you know." She gave a devilish grin. "De Palma was quoted as saying, 'If Angela is unavailable, well then, so am I.'"

"Angela ..."

"Yes, yes, I know. I'm obstructing justice again. My point is, that is why I ended up taking that god-awful part in the film, *Pennsylvania Dutch*. You know the one about the Amish women?"

I shook my head.

"Dear girl, do you watch *any* cinema?" she tutted. "Well, you are better off not having seen it. Terrible cinematography. We shot in Lancaster during some unusual rainy season, although the dreary weather fit right in with the project. To this day, that film remains one of the few blemishes, along with *Pop Goes the Damsel*, on my otherwise illustrious career."

Before I could redirect her, Angela continued. "Anyway, I took the role because it was the only one that would allow me to wear loose clothing, you see. Thank goodness Amish women have no sense of fashion. And the shoot was going to be a long six months in farm country. I believed I would be able to hide my pregnancy under those dreadful dresses and aprons."

"What does this all have to do with what was written on the suicide note?"

"I'm getting to that. Haven't you ever heard of exposition?" She shook her head sadly. "Anyhow, my plan worked to a tee. No one suspected I was pregnant, although it would have been so much better if Siskel and Ebert hadn't given *Pennsylvania Dutch Country* two thumbs down, but that's neither here nor there."

"You weren't showing toward the end of your pregnancy?"

"A bit. But nothing I couldn't hide with loose clothing. The gossip columnists just assumed I gained weight from eating lard, meat, and potatoes for half a year."

"So, you had the child?"

She nodded. "Yes. I was alone. In my home."

"What?"

"I couldn't risk having anyone know."

I thought of a young Angela lying on the floor of her bathroom having a secret baby. "Oh my God. What if you'd needed medical attention? What if you had a complicated birth?"

"It's funny how I didn't think of any of those things at the time. I saw myself as a strong, independent woman, and I believed I would handle the delivery as I would anything else. With confidence."

"You were brave."

"I was stupid. I thought that child was going to rip me in two. I was in labor for fourteen hours, all night long. Until, finally, I heard a powerful wail. When I looked down, I saw a tiny face looking up at me." Angela turned away from me, which seemed unheard of. Like turning your back to an audience while on stage. "I had expected to feel nothing. But I felt an instant connection. And an overwhelming desire to protect him."

"It was a boy?"

"Yes, a beautiful, healthy boy. But I simply couldn't raise him. I just couldn't."

"I'm not judging you."

"Well, then you would be the only one. I was young. Up and coming. Yes, I was becoming a name, but not quite there yet. Even if I had wanted to keep him, I didn't have any money and was living in an apartment that was the size of a closet—and not a big one. So, I pulled myself together, wrapped him up as best as I could, and hurried him in the dark of night to a church, and I left him on their doorstep."

I gasped. "Really? You just dropped him and left?"

"That had been the plan. I left a note."

Another jolt of electricity. *A note.*

Angela nodded, as if reading my mind. "It said, 'I'm so very sorry. But it is for the best. I hope you understand one day.'"

I sat there, stunned. Had Angela's murderer had this note in their possession? Was it a copy? How would the killer know what was on a note she left with her baby on a set of church steps years and years ago? "What happened next?"

"I had intended to go home and sleep for three days. But, instead, I sat near a tree and watched the front of that church. I was so tired. I didn't think I could ever be as tired as I was that day. Eventually, a priest arrived and discovered him, and then some nuns came and began gushing over him—how could they not? He was beautiful. It was then I knew I had done the right thing. I had given him a chance at life. A *real* life. I made some inquiries in the weeks that followed and discovered a poor but kind family took him in and adopted him. I, too, had come from a poor but kind family. As far as I was concerned, he would have a chance to be happy."

"So, no one ever knew you were pregnant?"

"Never. Well ..." She rolled her eyes. "A tell-all book was written about me in the early nineties. It had some god-awful name like *Unauthorized Angela*. Or was it *Angela, Unauthorized*? I can't remember. By then, I had become the belle of the theater and film world. A trio of Tonys. Four Emmys. A Grammy. Two Oscars. Not that I'm counting ..." She patted the gray curls behind her head. (Probably because she couldn't reach her back.) "I was one of the first EGOTs, you know. And some blood-sucking journalist looking to make a name for herself wrote that I had had a secret pregnancy and wrote about leaving the baby at the church. To this day, I still don't know how she knew." She sighed. "I denied the pregnancy, of course. I had to. There was no benefit to admitting to it. But the unauthorized biography got me thinking. I began to wonder what had become of ... well, the boy."

"Did you find out? Did he have the life you imagined?"

She shook her head. "Sadly, no. Despite well-meaning parents, he grew up to be an angry young man. Was in and out of prison. I blamed myself."

I stood up. "Why didn't you tell me all this before?"

"There was no reason to."

"But this child, this angry child, could have been the one who murdered you. Maybe he knew he was adopted. Maybe he read this tell-all book about your pregnancy and somehow made the connection that you were really his mother."

"You know, my dear, for a bed-and-breakfast proprietor, you are quite perceptive."

"How do you mean?"

"Well, one night, I was performing a revival of my one-woman show, *Always Angela,* in New York City—this was about fifteen years ago. And a man was sitting in the front row. I knew instantly when I saw him that it was the boy I had given birth to."

"Your son?"

She nodded. "What can I say? A mother knows. Same strong chin. Just like his mother." She said those last two words with pride. "But when he came backstage, I told security not to let him in."

"Why not?"

"In addition to that strong chin, I noticed his eyes. They were angry. They were accusing. I didn't know why he was there or what he wanted to tell me, but I instinctively knew it wouldn't be good."

I quickly did the math in my head. This abandoned son was probably middle-aged by now. There must have been at least two dozen middle-aged men attending the conference. Any one of them could have been him. Any one of them could have gotten onto the balcony and murdered Angela. Had I seen him? Spoken to him? "What was his name?" I asked.

"Solomon. He was named by the priest who found him. The family who adopted him kept the name. Last name was Adamski. A Polish family."

"Maybe there was a Solomon Adamski registered for the conference," I said.

"Clara—"

"Or would he use another name?"

"Clara—"

"Maybe he had his name *legally* changed."

"Clara, Solomon wasn't the one who murdered me."

"But ... how can you be sure?"

Angela gave a breathless sigh. "Because Solomon died in prison not long after he visited me that night."

Chapter 19

I STARED UP AT the ceiling of my hotel room, watching the fan spin.

Angela had told quite a story. I thought about the night she performed at the conference cocktail party. How the audience gazed upon her. How polished and elegant she was. How confident. No sign of the struggles. The heartache. The hard decisions. There was so much that people didn't know about a person. The Uber driver's words returned to me again. *Don't get distracted by the shiny penny.* Weren't we all? Distracted by the glamour? The fame?

I reached for my phone and looked up *Angela, Unauthorized* on Amazon. I read the book synopsis.

Most people know Angela Decatur as the sophisticated stage actress who started from nothing and became a world-famous star. But few know the real story of how she clawed her way to the top, stopping at nothing and for no one. The casting couches. The bribes. The demands. The success-at-all-costs philosophy. The secret child. Within these pages, you'll read the story of the real Angela Decatur for whom "Anything Goes" was more than just a signature song.

Yikes. The author of the book hadn't pulled any punches. The only thing worse than having to suffer through hardships was to do it on the public stage so that every move you made would be chewed on and debated by people you didn't know. For years to come.

I did an online search for *Angela Decatur* and was inundated with results. I scrolled the websites, but there was nothing beyond what was being called a suicide and what a slew of celebrities were posting in her honor. Then I tried *Angela Decatur baby*; another list of websites filled my phone screen, all of them mentioning the tell-all book, but nothing else about a baby. Angela hid her secret well.

My phone pinged as a text from Stephanie popped on my screen, asking me if I wanted to join her for dinner. I couldn't think about eating. I texted a quick thanks and told her I would catch up with her at breakfast.

Another ping. Followed by classical music.

William.

Dear Clara,

I think you will be very pleased with the installation of the high-definition television, as it is described on the carton in which it arrived. I cannot recall ever seeing something so large within a home. Mr. Wiggins's handyman, as you called him, placed a tiny device, resembling a phone, next to it along with an instruction manual that states that such a device is called a "remote control." More technology to learn. Fascinating. When do people of the twenty-first century sleep?
Sincerely,
William

William. How I missed him. His kind, gray face. His pale blue eyes. I began to type.

William, hi. I miss you. And Ghost Cat. And Boy. Looking forward to seeing you soon.

Moments after I clicked *Send*, more classical music.

Dear Clara,
You sound melancholy. Are you well?
Sincerely,
William

William could tell from thousands of miles away, from a simple text, that I was sad. Joe had lived with me for eight years and didn't even know when I had been suffering from the flu for two weeks. William must have been a wonderful husband.

William, I'm sorry. I didn't mean to worry you. I'm fine. Just having a weird day. I met a woman who told me a sad story today. A story about her son. I can't get his name out of my mind. Solomon Adamski. He died a while ago. And she doesn't have any more family. She seems so strong to me, but I can't help but think she's feeling lonely. I know what loneliness feels like, I guess. I'll tell you more when I'm home.

I pressed *Send* and was about to put my phone on the nightstand when there was more classical music.

Dear Clara,
I, too, know what loneliness feels like.
Sincerely,
William

Ugh. Of course he did. He had been haunting an old, vacant home for more than a century. Sadness was the opposite of what I wanted William to feel. From the day I met him, I had wanted to help him. Cheer him up. Clear his name, if only that doggone Taylor Hampton would do what he promised to do. I texted back quickly.

I know you do. But that's in the past, right? You've reminded me that we need to focus on the now. And on each other. I'll see you soon.

I hit *Send* and placed my phone on the nightstand. Then I curled up under the blanket, wishing I had Boy next to me, when there was another *ping* followed by classical music. I reached for my phone.

Dear Clara,

After having visited a very reputable (per your directive) online directory, I discovered there is an address for a Chester Adamski in the Las Vegas area not far from where you are boarding. Perhaps it is a relative and your friend need not be so sad.

Sincerely,

William

I stared at William's text. An address for a Chester Adamski? William was trying to help. How kind. What he didn't realize was that lots of people could have the same last name in a town or city and not be related. Unlike in the 1800s, when families—and extended families—mostly lived close to one another.

But maybe he was onto something. I did a quick search for Chester Adamski. William was right. He lived in Las Vegas. I mapped the address. Only a fifteen-minute ride from the hotel. Could this Chester Adamski really be a relative of Solomon's, as William suggested? A brother? Or nephew? Or son?

I made a mental note to check in with Kurt tomorrow morning to see if a Chester Adamski was attending the conference. If there was, he could have been the one to kill Angela. He had the access. And a motive—if he was acting on behalf of Solomon Adamski, who Angela said had appeared angry when she last saw him.

I placed my phone on the nightstand, snuggled under the blankets, and sighed, my mind swirling. Another night of tossing and turning was in front of me. When Sebastian referred to Las Vegas as the city that never sleeps, I never figured this was what he might mean.

Chapter 20

I TOOK THE ELEVATOR up to the twenty-seventh floor and hurried into the ballroom before breakfast was set to begin. Since the room was mostly empty, Kurt Walker was easy to find. He was standing near the coffee machines, instructing several of the servers. When he finished, I approached him.

"Excuse me, Kurt?"

He looked at me and smiled. "Ah, Clara Kelly. How can I help you?"

"I was just wondering if … well, I was wondering if you could tell me if anyone by the name of Chester Adamski is attending this conference."

"Chester Adamski?" Kurt thought for a moment and shook his head. "No, the name doesn't sound familiar. And I'd know. I make myself familiar with all the attendees. Why? Is he a colleague?"

"Oh, no, but I'm familiar with him and thought I'd introduce myself." Not a lie. "Thank you anyway."

As Kurt walked toward the pastry table, apparently satisfied with my non-answer, I scooted toward the balcony. Was it possible Chester Adamski *was* at the conference and had given a fake name? Or maybe he was a hotel employee? Angela was in her usual spot, watching me as I approached.

"Good morning," she said. "You look very glum. And very tired. Did our little field trip exhaust you?"

"I didn't sleep at all," I said.

"I must tell you, that's one thing I don't miss as a ghost," she said. "I was never fond of sleeping anyway."

"Does the name Chester Adamski sound familiar to you?"

She furrowed her thin eyebrows. "*Chester* Adamski? No, I'm afraid it doesn't. Is he a relative of Solomon's?"

"I don't know. I thought maybe he was registered for the conference, but Kurt Walker just told me he wasn't. He lives in Las Vegas, not far from here." I gave her the address. "Are you familiar with that location?"

"Not really. I never veered much from downtown Las Vegas, my dear."

I reached up and rubbed my compass pendant to help me think. I was running low on leads. Glenn Swanson was still in play. Could *he* be Chester Adamski? Or was he just a jerk I was trying to pin a murder on? "I'm thinking I should go check it out."

"Check what out?"

"The address. See if anything comes to me while I'm there."

"Another field trip? Would you like me to come with you?"

"No, that's all right. I'll be fast. It's about a fifteen-minute Uber ride from here." I looked at my watch. "I might miss most of breakfast, but I should be back for the end. I told my friend Stephanie I'd meet her."

"All right, then take a banana," Angela said. "A girl needs her potassium."

"Good idea. I need something in my stomach. I didn't eat last night."

"And take a bottle of water," Angela added.

"I was thinking coffee—and lots of it—but maybe you're right. Water for hydration to combat the Las Vegas heat."

"No, my dear. To help keep the wrinkles away. After all," she glanced at what were probably bags under my eyes, "it's never too early to start a skin care regimen."

As the Uber pulled in front of the address on my phone, I looked up at the home in front of me. It wasn't much different from the others around it. Maybe a little more run-down. Peeling paint. Hanging roof shingles and eaves. Large brown patches of grass in an otherwise overgrown lawn. The home looked ... unloved.

"Is there any possibility you can wait for me?" I asked the driver, who looked like he was barely drinking age. I had a feeling I knew the answer. It had taken forever to get this cab, and even longer to get out of downtown, and I hadn't been able to secure a round trip on the app. I smiled big on the off-chance he would take pity on me.

"Sorry," the kid said. "I have another fare after this one in ten minutes." As I looked back out the window at the house, he must have sensed my ambivalence. "But that fare's destination isn't too far from here. If I can, I'll try to circle back."

"Thank you," I said and stepped out of the car.

As he drove away, I looked at my watch. Not only had I missed breakfast by embarking on this little field trip, but also a big chunk of the morning session. Stephanie had texted me twice, but I hadn't texted her back yet. What could I say? That I was investigating a murder? *I* barely knew what I was doing here. It wasn't even ten a.m., and it was already roasting hot. Instead of baking in the morning sun, I should have been wearing a sweater in the frigid ballroom of my hotel, eating reheated scrambled eggs and sausage and teasing Stephanie about Declan. I unlatched the metal gate that led to the broken-brick pathway and walked toward the front door.

I pressed the doorbell, which elicited one of those old-fashioned *ding-dongs*, and waited.

And waited.

Great. No one was home. Why would there be? It was a weekday morning. Whoever lived here probably was at work.

Envelopes were sticking out of a small mailbox next to the door. I leaned forward so I could read the name on the first envelope. Chester Adamski. *Well, I'm in the right place.* I folded the first envelope down and read the name on a second envelope.

Karen Adamski.

Chester's wife, maybe? I folded down another letter and let out a tiny gasp.

Solomon Adamski.

Why was an envelope addressed to a person who had died years ago? Unless there was another Solomon Adamski living here. Or it was possible that Solomon Adamski *had* lived here and was still getting mail? My mother continued to get mail from all kinds of places *years* after she passed away.

I rang the bell again and tried to peek inside the house, but there was some kind of paper on the other side of the glass squares on the door, so I couldn't see anything. As I walked back toward the sidewalk and reached for my phone to call for another Uber, suddenly the front door opened. A young woman with short, wet hair was standing there like she had just taken a shower.

"Hi, can I help you?" she asked.

"Hi, is this Chester Adamski's residence?"

"Yes." She smiled. "But don't worry. I'm his sister."

Don't worry? A tea kettle whistle filled the air.

"Sorry," she said. "I have to get that. Come in."

She stepped away from the door, and I hesitated before going inside. The young woman seemed friendly enough and didn't give off a cold-blooded killer vibe. At least that's what my gut told me, but was it really possible to know these things for sure? And somehow she seemed like she was expecting me. Wasn't that weird? Or had I lost all sense of weird? I slowly went up the front steps and into the home.

Despite the rundown appearance of its exterior, the home was quite welcoming, albeit slightly messy with clothing hung from the backs of chairs and across tables. The woman who answered the door was heading toward me from another room.

"Sorry," she said. "My brother went out to get milk. I'm making us omelets. Today's his late day, and I thought I'd make us breakfast before my job interview this morning. Our schedules are so different. Like two ships passing in the night most of the time." She smiled. "He didn't tell me you were coming. Not that he ever does." She laughed. "I'm Karen, by the way."

"Clara. You have a lovely home," I said, my eyes drawn to a line of framed photographs on a fireplace mantel. (Was it *ever* cold enough to use a fireplace in Las Vegas?) One photo was of a man with his arms around two children, a boy and a girl. Was that man Solomon Adamski?

Above the photos, something was framed on the wall. An unfolded note, written on a yellowed piece of paper, under glass. I stiffened when I read the words: *I'm so very sorry. But it is for the best. I hope you understand one day.*

"That was my dad's," Karen said, motioning to the frame. "He was adopted. My birth grandmother left that note with him when she left him on the doorstep of some church way back when."

There it was. In the harried handwriting of a young, distraught mother. The words written on Angela's supposed suicide note.

"My father died of a drug overdose in prison," Karen said, but then covered her mouth with her hands. "Oh, sorry. I should have let my brother tell you. He's always accusing me of talking too much." She shrugged. "Anyway, my father was a good dad. Well, he tried. But he was very troubled. Always was. My mother helped keep him stable, but when she died fifteen years ago, I think it broke my dad." She gave a small smile. "I'm sure my brother didn't put all that on his dating profile. TMI."

"Fifteen years ago?" I asked. Solomon's wife died around the same time he went to visit Angela at her one-woman show? And then he died of a drug overdose in prison?

"Yeah. My brother had the note in his place, but when he moved back home a few months ago, he wanted to put it on the wall. He said he liked to look at it."

"Your brother?" I asked as an engine sounded from the open door, where a car was pulling into the driveway.

"Oh, here he is now." She turned toward the front door. "Chet, we have company!"

Chet?

When I turned around, a young man in a T-shirt was walking toward me, holding a carton of milk in his hand. I recognized him immediately.

My waiter from the conference's opening-night cocktail party.

The same waiter who helped a distraught Gabriela on the balcony.

Chet.

A nickname for Chester.

Chester Adamski.

Solomon's son.

Angela's grandson.

And, I knew now, her murderer.

Chapter 21

"It's about time. Did you milk the cows yourself?" Karen laughed and grabbed the milk from Chet's hand. "You're welcome to stay for breakfast, Clara." Her phone, which was in her back pocket, rang, and she pulled it out. "Oooh, I have to take this." She pressed the screen. "Karen speaking ... yes, it is ... I'm ... Oh, of course ... No problem. I'll be at my desk in two minutes." She clicked off the call. "Sorry. Job interview," she said to me. "The third one. A group interview. Keep your fingers crossed, Chet. I'll leave you with your friend." She dropped the milk container onto the table and ran upstairs. "She's cute, you know." Karen pointed to me. "And *nice*. Unlike the *last* one." Then she giggled as she disappeared out of sight.

Don't go, I wanted to yell. *Please.*

I could feel Chet's eyes on me as he stood in front of the open doorway, but I didn't want to give him a chance to say anything. *I need to get out of here.*

"Oh no, look at the time," I said, glancing at my watch. "I should get going, too."

"Do I know you?" Chet asked.

"No, I don't think so."

"Then why did my sister say I did?"

Um ...

"Wait, you look familiar." He looked at my red hair.

"I really have to go." I wasn't about to wait around for Chet's memory to kick in, but as I made my way toward the open door, he blocked it, a strange look on his face.

"Why don't you stay for a bit?" he asked.

"I really can't." *Think, think.* "I have a cab waiting for me."

"I didn't see one outside."

I couldn't stop looking at his hands. The hands that had taken the life from Angela Decatur.

"You look nervous," he said.

"I'm not." Lie.

"But you look it."

"Looks can be deceiving." Not a lie.

"I think I know why you're here," he said and *closed the door.*

Did he recognize me? If he did, would he try to hurt me? With his sister upstairs? I took a deep breath. "Why am I here?" I asked.

Chet sneered. "Like I would really say." But he didn't have to. I could tell by his expression that he knew I knew.

He took a step closer to me, and I instinctively took a step back. We were on opposite sides of the table, where the milk was sitting, condensation coating the sides of the carton. I glanced at the black jacket hanging over one of the chairbacks. The bottom of its sleeve had a button missing.

I knew where that button was. On the twenty-seventh-floor balcony of my hotel. Poor Angela, a seventy-something-year-old woman, had been no match for a young, strong Chet Adamski. And I wasn't sure I would be either.

"You're hard to forget with that red hair," he said, a smile spreading across his face. "I've seen you poking around the balcony on the twenty-seventh floor of the hotel. You have no business over there. Grandpa Adamski would have called you a *buttinsky*."

I watched him carefully, wanting to keep as much distance between us as possible. Chet had a gleam in his eye, the kind Joe used to have when he was about to lurch at me. He was going to make a move. I had to make one first.

I reached up and grabbed the framed note on the wall. Chet seemed aghast.

"Give that to me," he seethed.

"Let me out the door, and I'll leave it on the front steps," I said.

"You're not going to make it to the front steps."

"I'll scream."

"Maybe, but not for long."

"Your sister will hear."

"She'll understand." He glanced at the framed note in my hands. "Do you know she just *left* my father there on those church steps? Like he was a piece of garbage. She never wanted to be a mother."

He was talking. It wasn't exactly a confession, but I needed to keep him talking. More talking, less lurching. "She was young," I said. "And scared. Everyone does the best they can. They make the decisions they feel are best at the time."

"Does it seem right to you to throw away a child?"

"She didn't throw your father away. She took him to a church and waited around to make sure someone found him."

"How do you know she *waited around*?" He laughed. "There's no record of that."

He was right. There probably wasn't. "She told me. I know her pretty well."

"Knew." He smirked.

No, *know*. "And you're right. Angela Decatur never planned on becoming a mother. Didn't want to. But when she had your father, she told me she was overcome with love. But she was also so young and didn't think she could care for him."

We were circling around the table now.

"Do you know he went to see her one day?" Chet said. "He went to one of her performances. Saved up some money and got a front-row seat. He told me he could *tell* she knew who he was."

"She did."

Chet's eyebrows furrowed. "Well, then why didn't she see him backstage?"

"She said she couldn't face him." I decided to leave out the *angry eyes* part of the story.

He narrowed his gaze at me. "How dare you. How dare you *defend* that monster." He pointed to the framed note in my hands. "My father held onto that damn note his whole life, wondering if, maybe, one day, he might be able to talk to his mother about it, about why she left him. Then some book comes out, and he realizes that a famous and rich actress was his mother. Everything lined up. The town. The timing. The large clothing she was wearing during the filming of some movie. He *knew* it was her. And he was so angry at her. For leaving him. Giving him away just so she could have all that money for herself."

"I don't think that's why she did it. She didn't have a lot of money at the time." I took a small step toward the front door.

"He was *obsessed* with her. Turned to drinking. Drugs. And then ..." Chet shook his head. "After years and years, can you believe he just *forgave* her?" Tears formed in the crevices of his eyes. "At the end. When he was in prison. Karen and I went to visit him with our Grandma Adamski. He told us that he was wrong. That carrying hate in your heart only hurts yourself."

"He was right."

"He was *weak*. For years, I stared at that note." He motioned to the frame in my hands. "Every time he forgot to pick me up at school. Every time we didn't have money for a class trip. Every time we had tuna fish sandwiches for dinner for a week. I *memorized* that note. Every curve of the handwriting. Every crossed *T* and dotted *i*. That note ruined my father's life. And mine."

"I don't think it's that simple."

"It is for me. And she needed to pay. I took the stupid waiter job just to be close to the hotel she was performing in, waiting for my chance. And then it came." He smiled. "I found out she would be doing a private gig in the very hotel I was working in. If that's not fate, I don't know what is."

He darted around the table, and I threw the framed document at him, hoping to slow him down, and it fell to the ground, shattering. Then I ran toward the front door and was about to open it when Chet grabbed me from behind. His hands were strong, just like Joe's, and I envisioned him covering my nose and mouth, just like he had done to Angela. I screamed when suddenly the front door burst open, and a police officer yanked Chet off me.

I stood against the wall, gasping for breath and watching the big, bulky officer push Chet to the floor.

"Can you keep it down, people?" Karen yelled, running down the stairs, but she nearly fell down them when she saw what was happening.

"Are you okay, Miss?" Another officer was standing at the front door, talking to me. The name *Levy* was written on his uniform.

"He killed Angela Decatur." I pointed at Chet, and when I did, Karen's eyes grew wide. "It wasn't a suicide. He made it look like a suicide. He learned her handwriting and replicated the words on that note there on the floor in the shattered glass." The words were coming fast and furious. "He's Angela's biological grandson. He blamed her for his father's troubles. He's been working as a waiter in my hotel, where Angela was performing this week. If you check that jacket on the back of that chair, you might find Angela Decatur's DNA on it or something, if he hasn't washed it."

"She's lying," Chet shouted from the floor. I glanced at Karen, who was sitting on the bottom step of the staircase now, listening to me. I didn't know if she knew what Chet had done; my sense was that she was hearing all this for the first time. I pointed to the chair. "That jacket also has a button missing. You'll find it on the twenty-seventh-floor balcony of the hotel, which is where he killed her and then placed her body on the ledge to make it look like a suicide."

The officer holding Chet stopped what he was doing and stared at me. "How do you know all this?" he asked.

Good question. "I didn't know for sure. But what I did know was that Angela Decatur hadn't killed herself."

"How?" Officer Levy asked. "How did you know?"

Another good question. "I just ... knew ... *her*."

The officer brought Chet to his feet and cuffed his hands behind his back. "You have no right to detain me," Chet shouted. "She's lying."

"At the very least, you attacked this young woman," Officer Levy said. "We have every right to cuff you." He glanced at Karen and me. "And now I'd like us all to take a ride to the station so we can get to the bottom of things."

Officer Levy was about to walk over to Karen when I said, "Wait, I don't understand. How did you know I was here?"

Officer Levy pointed outside the front door.

I turned and there, standing alone at the bottom of the front stairs, pushing up on her large-rimmed glasses, was Alice.

"Alice?" I asked, stepping outside.

Alice's eyes found the ground, and she began using the toe of one of her white sneakers to trace a brown patch in the grass.

"How did you know I was here?" I asked.

"Stephanie was really worried. She said you skipped dinner last night and were supposed to meet her for breakfast. She tried texting you and didn't hear back." She reached up and tightened her ponytail at the back of her head. "I guess I was worried, too. So ..."

I waited for Alice to continue because I had a feeling I knew what she was going to say, and I couldn't believe it.

"I ..." Alice took a breath. "I went up to Angela's ghost by the balcony."

"You spoke to Angela's *ghost*?" I asked. "For me?"

She shrugged. "She was surprised I could see her. I told her you were gone, and she said you came here." She pointed to the house. "She gave me the address."

"I'm surprised she remembered the address." I walked down the front stairs. "I only mentioned it in passing."

"I said the same thing. But then she said, 'My dear, I've memorized *thousands* of lines of dialogue in my career. I think I can handle remembering an address.'"

I smiled a little. Then, to my surprise, Alice did, too. "That sounds like Angela," I said.

"I called 9-1-1 in case you were in trouble," Alice said. "The operator told me there was a police car right outside the hotel and that she would alert them, but I needed to go down myself. When I got there, Officer Levy told me there had been a lot of pranks lately, so I needed to go with them if I wanted them to check out my story. I guess they wanted to hold me accountable. I knew when I got into that police car there was a chance this was all a big misunderstanding and it would look like I was pranking them, too. But I had a feeling it wasn't."

"Ladies …" Officer Levy was standing at the front door as another police car pulled in front of the house. "If you don't mind getting into these officers' car, we'd like you to come to the station to make a formal statement."

"Of course, Officer," I said. "But does Alice have to come, too?"

"I don't mind," she said.

"Good," Officer Levy said. "Right this way then." He led us to the second police car.

As I got into the backseat, the other officer took Chet to the first car. He looked back at me with angry eyes. I couldn't help but think they were the same angry eyes leering at Angela Decatur from the front row of a theater fifteen years ago.

"You saved my life, Alice," I said as she sat next to me and Officer Levy shut the door.

"Well then, we're even," she said.

"What do you mean?"

She shrugged as the officer who was driving put the car in reverse and backed out of the driveway. "Because I'm starting to believe you might have saved mine, too."

Chapter 22

By the time I got to the twenty-seventh floor of my hotel and the elevator door opened, I was exhausted. It had been a long day at the Las Vegas Metropolitan Police Department, giving an official statement and waiting until the officers checked out my story. They found the black button right where I said it was located and took it, as well as Chet's waiter jacket, for evidence. Alice was with me the whole time, and Karen Adamski was there for her brother. Despite what had happened, they seemed close, and I wondered if they would continue to be. I was looking forward to dinner with Stephanie and the gang, but I just had one pit stop to make first.

Angela was standing in her usual spot, by the glass doors of the balcony.

"I'll miss this view," she said as I approached. She looked at me. "You found him, didn't you? The person who murdered me."

"Yes. How did you know?"

"Well, the police were here again. They took that button you photographed. And, I don't know ... a feeling, I guess. I feel *different*."

"It was Solomon's son. Chet. He was the one who murdered you."

"Chet?"

"He was a waiter here at the conference."

Angela shook her head sadly. "So, I was done in by a waiter who murdered me to avenge the dreadful life I had destined for his father when I abandoned him on a church doorstep. How utterly Shakespearean." She made the motion of sighing. "I'll never know if I did right by my son. By Solomon. All I know is that I did what I thought was best at the time."

"That's all any of us can do," I said.

Angela stood a little taller. "My word, you *are* a crime-solving savant, aren't you? Thank you for all you've done for me, Clara. I must say, I never had many female friends in my life. Perhaps I was too competitive with other women to have them. I don't know if the industry made me that way, or I was simply that way, but it is one of the great disappointments of my life."

"Well, you've made one female friend."

"Thank you, Clara. For everything." She furrowed her brows in concern. "Was it very scary? Your field trip this morning?"

"A bit. But I've had my share of run-ins with violent men."

"As have I," Angela said.

We nodded knowingly at one another. "My husband wasn't kind," I said.

"You know, this whole ordeal reminds me of a role I once played." Angela touched her gray finger to her chin.

"I had a feeling it would," I said with a smile.

"In the early nineties, I starred in the acclaimed film *Chivalry Isn't Ted* in which I played the long-suffering wife of a man named Ted—a brute of a man who got what was coming to him in the end. Did your husband get what was coming to *him*?"

"Let's just say he can't bother me anymore," I said.

"Good." She nodded and reached for my hand; I felt her touch a little. "Well, I feel my time here is coming to an end, my dear. Lord knows I have received unsolicited advice all my life from people who had no reason to give me advice, but I must tell you this before I go: Don't hide."

"I won't. I made a decision not to hide anymore from ghosts. I'm going to help them."

"I don't mean from ghosts. Certainly, none of us can hide from death, but so many of us hide from *life*. Be bold, my dear. Be daring in your life. We've only got one shot at this. I've been thinking a lot as I've stood here overlooking Las

Vegas." She motioned to the balcony window. "I should have seen Solomon when he came to see me. Despite my fears. Despite my misgivings. Fears hold us back. Keep us from becoming our whole selves. I was bold in my career. Not so much in my life offstage. There are some prisons we make for ourselves."

I thought of Alice, who had broken free from hers. Just in time to save me.

"I'm feeling all tingly," Angela said. "Perhaps this is goodbye."

"I think so."

"My earthly residency is coming to an end." Angela let go of my hand and walked slowly toward the stage that had been pushed off to the side of the ballroom that very first night of the conference. She stepped onto it, stood at the center, and turned to me. "I wish you much joy in your life, Clara Kelly. If there's one thing you can learn from an old broad like me, it's not to take any crap from anyone. *Especially* men. As my character, Victoria Milne, said in *Haddington Housewife*, that foreign film Hitch insisted I do ..."

"Hitch?"

"Alfred Hitchcock, my dear. You really *do* need to see more cinema." She cleared her throat. "Victoria said, 'When life hands you a bum, that's what he should land on when you kick him to the curb.'"

"I'll remember that." I plucked a long-stemmed flower from its vase on a nearby table and tossed it onto the stage at Angela's feet. "Brava," I said and clapped softly.

Angela smiled. Then, with the backdrop of Las Vegas behind her, she took one last dramatic bow and vanished.

Chapter 23

I PULLED MY LUGGAGE toward Stephanie's room with extra vigor. I was going home! With great relief, the rest of the conference had continued without any more drama (or murder), and I was eager to wrap my arms around my family and put into action all the things I'd learned during my trip—except for the marketing info, which was overwhelming and made me feel like I wanted to crawl under a blanket and never come out. *Baby steps.* I triple-knocked—a knock each for William, Boy, and Ghost Cat—on Stephanie's hotel door.

"Time to jet, Ms. Hastings!" I called. "I'm pretty sure Delta isn't going to hold the flight for us!"

When Stephanie didn't answer, I triple-knocked again and waited. There was a rustling sound coming from inside her room.

"If you're not ready," I said, "it's okay. I can—"

The door opened, and I tried not to look surprised as, instead of Stephanie standing there, Declan was running his hands through his bed-head hair. "Hi," he said, sheepishly. "Stephanie's in the shower. We're running a bit late."

Well, Stephanie got her slumber party after all. I smiled. "Oh, I'm so sorry. I didn't mean to disturb—"

"Nothing to be sorry about. The time just got away from us. We'll be down in ten minutes."

"Okay," I said. "I'll meet you downstairs. Oh, and I was just kidding about Delta. We have time, so don't rush." *Stop talking. He gets it.*

I wheeled my luggage toward the elevators and pushed the down button, taking one last look around the hotel hallway. How ironic that all my life I had wanted to travel, but at this moment, all I was looking forward to was getting back to my little place in the world. Salem, Massachusetts. And snuggling next to Boy with a good book. And Ghost Cat, too, if she was in the mood. Texting with William had been fun, but there was nothing like having him standing in front of me, adjusting his military jacket and gazing at me and the world with his warm, pale blue eyes. That Dorothy Gale knew what she was talking about. There definitely was no place like home.

Downstairs, slot machines were beeping and gamblers were shouting, but somehow it didn't seem as loud as it had been when I first arrived. Had I gotten used to the noise?

Near the checkout desk, the conference attendees were bunched in groups, and I made my way toward Sissy, Jonah, and Alice, whom I almost didn't recognize. Her dark hair was no longer in its usual ponytail and was framing her face with a slight wave. Alice seemed to finally be letting her hair down. And I was glad.

"Have you seen Stephanie and Declan?" Sissy asked when I reached them.

I was about to say they were going to be a few minutes late when Sissy pointed and said, "Oh, there they are."

I turned around to see them coming toward us, holding hands. *Awww!* While Las Vegas had been a certain kind of trip for me—to start traveling again, to learn some business tips, to solve a murder—Las Vegas had been quite another kind of trip for them.

"What's going on?" Stephanie asked when she reached us. "People seem to be chattering about something."

"Didn't you hear?" Jonah asked.

"Hear what?" I asked.

"Angela Decatur was *murdered*," Sissy whispered.

Alice and I glanced at each other.

"Just terrible," Sissy said, her deep brown eyes sad.

"Who killed her?" Stephanie asked.

"I heard it was one of the waiters," Jonah said.

"One of the waiters?!" Stephanie asked, alarmed. "You mean, the waiters who had been around us all week serving us croissants and coffee?"

"Yeah, but the waiter was a long-lost grandson or someone," Jonah said. "There was some kind of bad blood in the family. I'm not sure."

I was sure. And so was Alice. But neither of us was saying anything.

"So, he pushed her off the balcony?" Stephanie asked.

"Allegedly," Declan said, which caused Jonah to laugh.

"Why are you laughing?" Sissy asked.

"You know … A-*ledge*-edly." Jonah looked at us. "Too soon?"

"Well, I, for one, feel terrible," Sissy said. "Angela hadn't jumped at all, and I got caught up in all the speculation, as much as I tried not to. She was taken from us before her time and had so much more to give the world."

"I'm still trying to get over the fact that a murderer was walking around up there serving us refreshments," Stephanie said. "No wonder everyone is whispering to one another."

"Well, they're whispering about that and something else," Jonah said.

"There's *something else*?" Stephanie asked. "Well, don't just stand there. Out with it."

"Well," Jonah said dramatically, as if he was taking his cues from Angela. "You know that guy—"

"Get your hands off me!"

At the far end of the checkout desk, Glenn Swanson was shouting at two men who were ushering him through the lobby.

"I don't need an escort," Glenn was saying as the conference attendees parted like the Red Sea to let him pass.

"What's happening?" I whispered.

"That's what I was trying to tell you," Jonah said. "That guy right there ..."

"The guy who was hitting on Clara?" Stephanie asked.

Jonah looked at me. "He was hitting on you?"

"That's not important," I said. "What happened?"

"Well, that guy, Glenn Something, and Kurt Walker's wife were getting it on during the opening-night cocktail reception."

"No!" Stephanie said.

"Yes," Jonah said. "From what I hear, that guy has been to a few of these conferences, and let's just say he's not here for the business advice."

"You mean they've done this before?" Declan asked.

"Yep. Several times. The night that Angela Decatur was murdered, I heard they were in the men's bathroom."

"Ewww," Stephanie said.

"How terrible," Sissy said. "Didn't Kurt Walker say this week was he and his wife's tenth wedding anniversary?"

"He did," I said, watching Glenn Swanson head toward the large front doors of the casino. I knew he had been lying about where he was during Angela's murder. I just didn't know about what.

The chatter among the conference attendees heightened again as Kurt Walker and his wife, Deidre, walked into the lobby from the elevator bank. Kurt wasn't looking as lovingly at his wife as he had been all week. It was clear they had been fighting.

Stephanie's phone pinged. She looked at the screen. "Our Uber's outside. And I made sure our driver isn't the depressing guy who drove us here."

"I didn't mind that guy," I said.

"Let's just say he had a rain cloud over his head, and I didn't bring my umbrella," Stephanie said with a laugh and pulled Declan toward the revolving front door of the hotel. I was about to follow along when I felt a tap on my shoulder and turned. Stanley Paulson was standing in front of me.

"Clara Kelly," he said. "I'm glad I caught you before you left."

"Stanley, hi. I'm so sorry I wasn't able to make your second session this week." *Please don't ask me why.*

"That's fine. You didn't miss much, although I'd love to talk more about your new bed-and-breakfast." He paused, looking slightly uncomfortable. "It looks like my schedule will take me to the Boston area sometime soon. Is it all right if I look you up when I'm in town?"

"Yes, that would be great. I'd like that."

He smiled, appearing relieved. "Maybe the Kensington House Bed-and-Breakfast will be up and running by then, and I can stay at your place and learn a thing or two."

"I don't know about that." I laughed. "Opening for business, right now, seems so far away."

"You'll get there, Clara. It was nice seeing you." He stuck out his hand, and I shook it. "Safe travels."

"You too," I said, watching him go. I caught Stephanie looking back at me on her way out the door, and she was making a kissy face. I made a funny face at her and began walking behind Alice and Jonah, who were chatting, when there was another tap on my shoulder.

"I see you were able to break through with Alice," Sissy whispered into my ear, pointing at Jonah and Alice. "I'm glad. She needs a friend. And I can't think of a better one." She gave me a soft hug and then walked ahead as the concierge waved goodbye.

"Come back and see us soon," he said as we walked outside into the dry, high heat of Las Vegas.

I looked up at the Sphere, which was decked out in red, white, and blue, resembling the American flag, and the rest of the buildings around me. Maybe one day I'd come back to this big, loud, busy town. There was so much I didn't get to see and do. But right now, it was time to feed my dog, pet my ghost cat, and chat for hours with my best friend. It was time to go home.

Chapter 24

"Thﾒe's my little guy!"

Boy pushed his paws up against the corral gate at the back of The Pampered Pup. His curly little tail was wagging fiercely, and he was wearing a very debonair little tuxedo vest to go with his black bowtie hair clip.

"Well, hello, traveler!" Sebastian said as he came out of the back room.

"Hey, Sebastian!" I reached down and picked up Boy, cradling him in my arms. He licked my cheeks, my chin, and the tip of my nose.

"Somebody is happy to see you," Sebastian said.

"I'm not sure who's happier, Boy or me," I said.

Sebastian reached under the counter and pulled out the bag I had left with all of Boy's things. "I've gathered all his stuff together. His toys, what's left of his food. He was such a good boy, Clara. He's really a sweetheart."

"I know." I hugged Boy again. "Thank you for taking such good care of him."

"My pleasure. Did you have a good trip?"

How to answer that? "Yeah, I think I did. I learned a lot. About traveling. About business. About Las Vegas." I laughed. "And, I guess, about myself. And I also made some new friends." I thought of Alice.

"Sounds perfect."

"Yeah. I'm excited to get home, though. I had some renovations done while I was gone, and I'm eager to see what it all looks like. I'm a little nervous that it'll be different, you know?"

"Yeah, change is hard. But it's also exciting."

"Yeah." I stood there with Boy in my hands, watching Sebastian. Sweet, kind Sebastian. With his messy, dirty-blond hair. Those dreamy green eyes that sparkled. That cute freckle on his forehead. The clothing perpetually full of dog hair.

"Is everything all right, Clara?"

Angela's final words appeared in my mind. Like a neon sign. *Be bold. Be daring.*

"Clara?" Sebastian asked.

The nervous knot in my belly grew tighter. Joe was gone, really gone, and I didn't want him to linger anymore. In how I chose to live my life. In the decisions I made. Sebastian was right. Change *was* good. And exciting. And it was time for more change. "Sebastian?"

"Yes?"

"I was thinking ... would you like to have dinner with me? Maybe in a week or two? Once I get settled?"

Sebastian's green eyes lit up, and he broke into a smile. "Yes, I would like that very much."

"Great." Relief flooded through me like water through a dam—a dam that had been built brick by brick over eight years and was finally sprouting holes. "Do you want to try Salem Seas? It's a new restaurant. Jonah Duncan is the owner. I met him on the trip to Las Vegas."

"Sure, sounds perfect." He smiled.

"What? Why are you smiling?"

"It's funny," he said. "You're the one who went to Las Vegas. But somehow, I'm the one who feels like a winner."

My cheeks warmed. "Well, I'd better go and get this little guy home. I'll talk to you soon?"

"Sounds good." He reached into the bag on the counter for Boy's harness and leash. "Do you need these?"

"Nah, I think I'll carry him to the car." I didn't want to let him go. "See you soon."

I grabbed Boy's things and left The Pampered Pup, excited to be once again on the cobblestone streets of Salem, Massachusetts. My hometown. And as I snuggled Boy in my arms, I waved one last time to Sebastian and, for the first time in a long time, wondered what it might feel like to have *another* boy in my arms to snuggle with.

Chapter 25

When I walked into Kensington House, I barely recognized the home I was standing in. The dining room walls were painted a warm light blue, the kitchen a lovely crème, and the flooring shined, the faint smell of lacquer still in the air. It was amazing what a simple paint or stain job could do to a space.

"Clara, you've returned." William appeared at the entrance to the living room, wearing a toolbelt. He must have seen me looking at it; his cheeks tinged a dark gray as he removed it and placed it on a side table. "One of the laborers left this behind. Just trying it on for size. Are you content with the work that's been done?"

"The house looks amazing, William." I placed Boy on the newly varnished wood floor, and he slipped and slid right to his bed, which William must have placed back in its usual spot. Boy picked up my blond wig and began gnawing on it, picking up right where he left off. "And you handled everything so well. Really, it was such a relief to have you here while I was traveling. I knew Kensington House was in good hands."

The corners of William's mouth curved upward. "Did you gain much knowledge at your event?" he asked.

"Yeah, but I think I learned most of all that my favorite place in the world is right here with you, Boy, and Ghost Cat."

"I see your noble nature and sunny disposition has been unchanged by the change in air pressure," William said as Ghost Cat sauntered in through the front door.

"Well, hello, my beautiful painters-tape-loving girl," I said.

Ghost Cat was about to walk right past me when she spotted Boy. Instead of walking away coyly as she usually did, she headed right toward him. Then, to my surprise, she curled up next to him and rubbed her head against his leg as he gnawed on the wig. *Awww, she missed him!*

"Do you require assistance with your bags?" William asked.

"Nah, I'm going to leave them for now, but I want to see if the Wi-Fi is working." I placed my briefcase on my new antique desk, also back in its usual spot, and pulled out my laptop, plugging it in. "There was so much emphasis on marketing at the conference, and I have to say, I'm a bit intimidated."

"There is a small placard on the table for the computer." William pointed to a business card that read *admin Wi-Fi password*. "It was left by the internet technician."

"Perfect." I inputted the password and was happy when my computer connected. "Yay, it works! I realized on the plane that I hadn't looked at my email all week. According to one of the networking sessions I attended, I'm supposed to get into the habit of checking it regularly and staying in touch with customers when I can."

"Oh?" William was studying me.

"I had gotten quite a few subscribers to my list after my Wyatt House sponsorship. The experts say I should have already been in contact with them, letting them know how preparations are going on the bed-and-breakfast—you know, giving them special access, an inside look at the renovations or something like that." I shook my head. "This is all so new to me. My marketing classes in college didn't really cover any of this."

"You will do fine, Clara," William said.

"Thanks," I said, looking at my email. "Wait …"

"Is something troubling you?"

I stared at the screen. "This can't be right."

"What cannot be right?"

"It says here I have almost a thousand subscribers."

"Is that incorrect?"

"It must be. I only had a couple of hundred after my Wyatt House event. Somebody must have made a mistake." I scrolled. "My email inbox is filled with responses. Responses to what?" I scrolled some more. "Wait, these responses aren't to *my* email address. They're to *yours*."

William's gray cheeks darkened. "While you were away, I did some internet research—only going to reputable websites, of course. They noted that, as you related, engaging with your email list benefits business in the twenty-first century. As you had your days occupied on the other coast of the United States, I thought I could assist."

"Assist?" I clicked on one of the email threads:

William,

How wonderful to meet you! Thank you so much for your reply to my email. It's been a long time since I've received a correspondence that had been so thoughtfully composed. I will definitely be staying at Kensington House during my next visit to the northeast, and I will be telling all my friends about your lovely bed-and-breakfast. Enjoy the rest of your summer!

Sincerely,

Wilma Kovacs

Gosh, what had William written? Knowing him, whatever it was would be polite and helpful. I scrolled down the email thread to William's email.

Mrs. Kovacs,

You've inquired about staying at Kensington House Bed-and-Breakfast in the off-season, and I can assure you there is much to see and do in Salem in all seasons. I have lived here all my days, and my favorite times were of a simple nature: picnicking in the park in the springtime, walking amidst the grandiosity of the fall foliage of autumn, watching the ships come and go as the winter chill nibbles at the tip of my nose, and, of course, the wonder of summer as I walk along the cobblestone streets and admire the colonial architecture. I look forward to the pleasure of your patronage.

Sincerely,

William Kensington

"William, this is wonderful."

"I read on my telephone device that it is proper to welcome members to an email list and to tell them a little about yourself or the town they're interested in. Many of them responded they would tell their friends about Kensington House and also list us on various organization pages."

"Oh my gosh, you attached a photo of the new painted walls and flooring in the living room, showing our progress. You did exactly what we're supposed to do." I couldn't believe it. I clicked on another email.

William,

How wonderful to meet you! Thank you so much for all the information about Kensington House. Will you have availability in the winter?"
Joanne Andres

And another one.

Dear William,
This is the most wonderful email reply I've come across, and I'm a regular traveler. I believe you'll do well. Best of luck with your new bed-and-breakfast.
Kind regards,
Matthew Edwards

"That settles it, William," I said.

"Settles what?"

"You can be my business partner!"

"Business partner?"

"As this trip to Las Vegas showed me, I find marketing very overwhelming, but you were able to provide personalized messages to hundreds of prospective guests over the course of a week. That's *amazing*. The job is yours, but only if you're interested. No pressure."

"What does such a job entail?"

"What you're already doing. Keeping in touch with customers. And giving them whatever information you like. I trust your judgment. What do you think?"

"It would be my pleasure to assist you."

"Great. We'll figure out compensation later."

"Compensation? There is none needed, Clara."

There was *no way* I would ask William to help with the bed-and-breakfast without giving him something in return. What did ghosts value most? I'd have to figure it out.

William's gray finger reached down and began deftly scrolling on my laptop. He seemed to have learned quite a bit about navigating the internet while I was gone. He clicked on a message. "You might find this particular correspondence of interest," he said.

William,

I'm so excited to hear that your bed-and-breakfast will be up and running soon. Although part of me will always cherish the night Wayne and I stayed there when the rooms were full of dust and there was no electricity. I'm hoping that all the renovations will not have scared away your friendly neighborhood ghost! (Ha!) Anyway, it sounds like Clara hired a very capable person to help her run the place, and I look forward to meeting you.

Signed,

Cindy (and Wayne)

"You were in touch with Cindy!" I said. "Little does she know that *you're* the friendly neighborhood ghost and that you already met." I smiled and closed my laptop. Boy was next to me, his paws on my legs. I picked him up. "C'mon, let's go check out our new television."

The color I had picked out for the living room was perfect, a color not much different from the darkish blue wallpaper that was there before. The television was on a stand on the wall adjacent to the library. I imagined cozy chairs surrounding it, with coffee and side tables. I'd have to go shopping for furniture next. I picked up the remote control and sat on the old, dusty sofa, placing Boy beside me. I clicked the button and the screen lit up.

"Oh!" William exclaimed as images appeared and music from a menu channel came on. "Will we require shades for our eyes?"

I giggled. "I don't think so," I said and scrolled through the listings.

"What do all those words denote?" he asked.

"These are all the programs that are on TV right now," I said.

"So great a number?"

"You wouldn't believe how many." I kept scrolling. "There are sports games and matches from all over the world. Old movies. New movies. Cooking shows. Game shows. Anything you want to watch, and ... oh my gosh!"

"What is the matter?"

"There's an Angela Decatur movie marathon on."

"Angela Decatur?"

"She's the woman I met in Las Vegas. She's the one whose murderer you helped me to find."

"Murderer?" William looked befuddled.

"I'll tell you all about it tomorrow, promise." I scanned the TV screen. "I wonder which film of hers is playing now. Oh, it's *Chivalry Isn't Ted*. She told me about this one."

"I read in an internet publication that popcorn is often enjoyed while viewing motion pictures."

"That's true," I said with a laugh.

"Shall I fetch some?" William asked. "I believe there is some in the cupboard."

Kind, thoughtful William. How I missed him. "No, thank you. I'm fine."

"And what about *you*?" he asked.

William was looking at Boy, whose tail began to wag.

Bark!

"I think that's a yes," I said with a giggle.

"Indeed. The hound has never met a meal opportunity he hasn't taken. I'll see what I can find that does not include chocolate or onions."

"Chocolate or onions?"

"Another internet publication explained those are not suitable for canines."

William left the room, and I snuggled next to Boy, happy to be home in the town I loved, with the family I loved. I clicked to Angela's movie and increased the volume. How young she looked. And yet the same. As she walked across the screen, I was reminded of the way she promenaded across the twenty-seventh floor of my hotel. With authority. And class.

"You ready to watch *Chivalry Isn't Ted*?" I asked Boy, who spun around until his back was against me.

Bark!

William returned, followed by Ghost Cat. He handed a treat to Boy, who gobbled it up and then reset himself as Ghost Cat sat beside him. Then William took a seat in the nearby club chair.

"It is a comfort to have you home, Clara Kelly," he said with a nod and then began gazing at the screen, his pale blue eyes not sure where to look.

"It's good to *be* home, William Kensington," I said, increasing the volume of the television as on-screen Angela spoke into a telephone.

"Everyone *knows* chivalry isn't Ted," Angela bemoaned with a disdain I recognized as the camera zoomed into her young, beautiful face.

Angela was right, of course.

Chivalry definitely wasn't Ted.

Because it was clear to me—since the day I met him—that chivalry was the man seated across from me with the wide-eyed look of wonder on his gray face.

Chivalry was William.

My friend.

And business partner.

Want more Clara and William? Get *G Is for Ghost*, Book 5 in the Salem Spirits Cozy Mysteries series, and read how their story continues!

Sign up for Dina Marie's email newsletter and get a Salem Spirits Cozy Mysteries short story for free! (Maybe even *two* free short stories!) Visit dinamariebooks.com for details.

About the Author

DINA MARIE IS THE pen name of award-winning novelist Dina Santorelli, who has been obsessed with all things ghost since . . . well, forever. Married on Halloween, she likes vacationing in spooky cities and visiting cemeteries and haunted hotels. A recent visit to Salem, Massachusetts, inspired her Salem Spirits series, which she wrote, in part, for her mom, a lover of cozy mystery TV.